Paul Charles

agent, promoter, author and fan of The Beatles, was born in Magherafelt, Northern Ireland. *Last Boat to Camden Town* is his second novel and the third – another Christy Kennedy mystery, *Fountain of Sorrows* – is nearing completion.

Last Boat to Camden Town

Paul Charles

BLOODLINES

First Published in Great Britain in 1998 by
The Do-Not Press
PO Box 4215
London SE23 2QD

First edition

ISBN 1 899344 30 6 – Paperback

British Library Cataloguing in Publication Data. A catalogue record for
this book is available from the British Library.

h g f e d c b a

Printed and bound in Great Britain by The Guernsey Press Co Ltd.

This book is dedicated to the memory of
Russell and Leslie Charles

Special thanks to Ann McGarvey for words on wards, to Christina Czarnik for words in the office, to Paul Fenn for long time words, to Jim Driver for words above and beyond, to Andrew & Cora for parental words and to Gillian and Jonathan for good words.

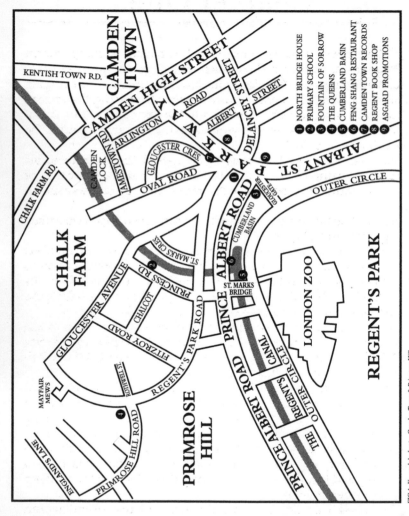

FIG 1: Kennedy's beat – Camden Town & Primrose Hill

1. NORTH BRIDGE HOUSE
2. PRIMARY SCHOOL
3. FOUNTAIN OF SORROW
4. THE QUEENS
5. CUMBERLAND BASIN
6. FENG SHANG RESTAURANT
7. CAMDEN TOWN RECORDS
8. REGENT BOOK SHOP
9. ASGARD PROMOTIONS

Chapter One

'Shit, not six already!' hissed Martin Shaw as he flung his arm out from under the bed covers. He groped at the open space in the general direction of the loud disturbance – the ringing alarm clock – in a desperate bid to silence it. Missing the snooze button (only just) he sent it tumbling to the floor and rolling out of reach (only just). 'These mornings are arriving earlier and earlier,' he complained to the clock.

'Not true, your nights are leaving later and later,' murmured his companion, using all her concentration to remain in some sort of sleepy humour. 'Stop making such a racket before you wake me up completely.'

'Sorry,' Martin whispered, 'but it's no fun getting up at this time.'

'Just shut up and get out!'

Leaving her to another few hours peaceful slumber, he grabbed his clothes and quietly exited the bedroom. After offering his face to a brief cat-lick, he scrubbed his teeth until blood flowed from his gums, the ice-cold water he used for rinsing his mouth shocking the last remaining sleep from his head.

No time for breakfast or newspaper or any such early morning civility. All such luxuries would have to wait another three hours until the longboat, the Sailing Diamond, came to a halt at the terminus of the first of its five daily trips.

Darkness still protected Camden Town as Martin left his flat in Arlington Road, his half-way house these last five years. He jogged up Parkway, passing the newsagents, breakfast shops, dry cleaners, estate agents (lots of estate agents), pet shop, banks, pubs and cafés – all silently working their way up through the gears of the morning – before crossing in front of the police station that was once a monastery and heading up Prince Albert Road, leaving the whisper of Parkway behind him.

He slowed to a walk as he passed the floating restaurant moored alongside Water Meeting Bridge which spanned the Regent's Canal, his place of work. Taking a left towards the zoo and then a quick right down a steep embankment, he passed through the gate leading to a little wooden hut in Cumberland Basin.

Junior, as usual, was already aboard, readying the longboat for the trip to the passenger pick-up point at Little Venice, a thirty-minute journey up the canal. Junior had been called Junior all his forty-three years on the planet. Junior's dad was also called Junior. Martin had long since given up trying to work out how complicated life must have been in the early years, when both Juniors lived in the one house. When the name 'Junior' was called, did Junior Senior or Junior Junior come running?

'Ah come on, Martin – get yer finger out. I don't wannabe late,' Junior said, smiling with the relief Martin knew was based on the fact that they would be at the pick-up point on time.

'Yeah, yeah, don't get your what's-its in a twist.'

Martin and Junior were used to each other's ways, and so silently got on with their jobs, readying the boat for its first voyage of the day. The Sailing Diamond, ninety-six years old and colourfully painted with bright blues, yellows and greens, looked as if it could have been owned by a circus. The name came from the time when it was the jewel in the crown of the second fleet of longboats built at the turn of the century by Thomas Pickford of City Basin. Originally horse-drawn, the boat was used then to cart materials to various craftsmen and dealers on the canal's eight-and-a-half-mile length. During the Second World War it transported munitions. Eventually, like its fellow longboats, it lost the battle to the London railway system and ceased to be a useful force on the canal.

For the twenty years between the end of the war and the rebirth of Britain in the Sixties, the Sailing Diamond was in dry dock at Kentish Town. Another twenty years passed and, after many coats of paint, it became the property of Turner Marinas – the present owner and employers of Junior and Martin. The boat, fifty-four feet long, could seat thirty-eight people but was rarely worked to capacity.

Martin readied the seats by wiping off the morning dew and replacing the multi-coloured cushions. Meanwhile, Junior primed the engine, bringing it up to tip-top condition for the day's efforts. After a while they were ready to cast off. Martin climbed on to the bank, released the ties and hopped back aboard. Junior engaged the engine and they slowly departed Cumberland Basin.

Martin had just resumed his work when he heard a loud splash to the aft – the blunt end. His first thought was that Junior had fallen overboard. The cushions scattered over the floor as he scrambled to the rear of the boat, doing his best not to panic. Looking up at the wheelhouse, he could see Junior – oblivious to Martin's concern – his pipe and the engine involved in some kind of unconscious smoke-raising competition.

'What the hell was that?' Martin shouted.

Junior was alarmed by Martin's worried look. 'What was what?'

'The splash. Shit, I thought you'd fallen overboard!'

Junior evidently had not the slightest idea what Martin was

raving on about.

Martin stared into the boat's wake, it's 'signature', created by the disturbance in the river of the powerful propeller. 'About a minute ago, just after we'd cast off – I could have sworn something fell overboard.'

His eyes scoured the grey water unsuccessfully. He saw – or thought he saw – air bubbles rising to the surface but they were now too far away for him to be certain. 'You're sure nothing fell off, Junior? I can't believe you didn't hear that splash.'

'Nothing – no, nothing. Jesus Martin, I can't hear anything up here with all the racket from the engine. Anyway, how many times have I told you not to come to work without breakfast? The hunger obviously makes you hallucinate.'

Martin was bewildered, then unsure, then lost. 'Ah well, I'd better get a move on. We're nearly there.'

The smoke from Junior's pipe, entwined with the plume of diesel fumes from the engine, slowly sank towards the water in an arc tracing their journey.

Chapter Two

All eyes were glued to his hand. It hung down by his left leg, as left hands have a habit of doing, and continuously, slowly and systematically, opened and closed. Stretching the fingers to their extreme and then, starting with the smallest digit, he recoiled each finger and finally the thumb into a fist. He repeated the process and seemed to take most relief – or pleasure – when he was stretching his fingers to their apex.

'What have we got here, then?' the owner of the stretching hand inquired.

'Well, sir,' began the young detective constable nervously, 'it seems like a suicide.'

His inquisitor's face gently creased into a well-worn smile. 'No, that's not the way we do it.'

Because of the smile, it was not taken as a reproach. Instead, the DC was now eager for the warm, soft voice to advise him further.

'First we work out, as best we can, what happened. We'll need assistance to fully ascertain this. We have – as you can see – a full team of experts here and there's a lot more waiting in the wings. The second thing we do is to find out the name of the deceased and as much about them as we can. Next we find out why whatever happened, happened to this person. Okay? What, Who and Why.'

He paused for a few seconds while his eyes survey the scene unfolding before and around him, his left hand flexing again.

'Then, and only then, detective constable, will we be in a position to know what really happened. When we reach that point we have a chance of figuring out the perpetrator of any crime that may have been committed.' Satisfied that this was now properly understood, Detective Inspector Christy Kennedy beckoned to his young assistant to accompany him down the grass slope towards the river. 'And perhaps now, you can help me solve a simpler mystery by telling me *your* name?'

'Detective Constable Ian Milligan, sir.'

'You've just transferred from Wimbledon, haven't you?'

'Yes, sir, arrived today. It's my first day in CID.'

'Wimbledon – a-ha, I see.'

Kennedy could keep the chat up no longer. He had delayed for as long as possible the inevitable – the inspection of the dead body.

Eighteen years on the force and the sight of a corpse still made his stomach churn. He had even thrown up on more than one occasion. Kennedy had never been able to fully understand his feelings. He wasn't exactly squeamish – at least, no more than the next guy. But then the next guy doesn't usually get to peer into the face of a body that has been robbed of life. Kennedy would choke with sadness as he contemplated the sad remains of somebody's father, somebody's son, somebody's mother – a person with dreams unfulfilled.

What he now saw before him on the bank of the canal was a well-dressed, well-fed male – probably aged in his late twenties. The body looked as if it had not long been in the water – hours, not days, he reckoned. Kennedy was happy about that much. The colder the corpse, the harder the hunt – that was his motto.

'Who found the body, Milligan?' Kennedy asked quietly, as he forced himself to further scrutinise the lifeless carcass.

'A longboat worker – Mr Martin Shaw, sir. That's him over there – the one wearing the black Pogues T-shirt, sir.'

'I'd like to speak to him first. And make sure this area is kept clear until the pathologist has had a chance to examine the body.'

Kennedy's voice betrayed his emotions – his words hardly audible to DC Milligan, who strained to catch his superior's order.

'Yes sir,' he replied, relaxing a little on realising that the detective inspector was, at the very least, human and, what's more, probably from the same planet as himself – something you didn't find too often in today's Metropolitan police force.

For himself, Kennedy was glad that his stomach had at least stopped shouting at him, the volume dropping to a mere mutter, though it would take some time before it quietened altogether.

'So then, Mr Shaw – who are the Black Pogues?' he asked the longboatman. Kennedy had found over the years that witnesses remember more when they're relaxed and it was his practice to begin the conversation by talking about anything other than the facts of the case.

'What?' Martin replied in disbelief.

'This shirt of yours – my DC told me it has to do with the Black Pogues.'

'They're more like the green Pogues. They're a group who would like to be Irish.'

'Oh, I see,' Kennedy replied, though not fully comprehending. 'My DC also tells me that you're the one who discovered the body. Would you mind telling me about it?'

Martin was totally thrown by the man – quiet and polite are not the usual attributes of senior police officers.

'Early this morning , just as we were casting off for the first trip, I heard this really loud splash. It had been on my mind all morning so when we took a break I decided to try and see what had caused it. It had seemed to come from near our moorings and if it was a bag of rubbish – as is often the case around here – I didn't want it getting jammed up in our propeller. The canal is only four feet deep over there.' Martin pointed to the moorings about twenty yards back up the bank from where the corpse lay.

'Okay, just stop there for a second.' It was something Kennedy did quite often, making time and space to digest facts, being careful not to misread the way someone said something, in case it veered him off in the wrong direction.

He stared at the water. It looked so harmless, yet it possessed the ability to end your very existence. You could try and pick it up and it would innocently fall though your fingers.

'So you wanted to make sure whatever it may have been that caused the loud splash was not going to interfere with your propeller. Is that right?'

'Yes. Exactly. I used a pole to poke around in the water. It's much too dirty to see anything. I'd all but given up. I'd worked my way up the bank to here, when I struck something solid. At first I thought it was a sack 'cos I could feel it give. But it seemed either too heavy for a rubbish-bag, or else I thought it might have been stuck to something. So I called to Junior and he fetched a pole as well and we heaved and pulled at it. Eventually it gave way and we dragged it towards us. When the head first emerged from the water we both let go of our poles and fell back on to the bank. I ran up over the bridge to the main road to ring for the police and saw that copper walking along...' Martin was pointing in the direction of a uniformed officer, currently engaged in crowd-control. '...He radioed for help and we hauled the body out. I've been shaking ever since.'

'Have you any tea-making facilities on the boat, Martin?'

'Yes – yes, of course,' came the quavering reply.

'Good. It's my experience in these matters that there is nothing as good for the shakes as a strong cup of tea – with lots of sugar.'

This was all a bit new for Martin. 'Okay, sir – sure. Why not?'

'And do one for me while you're at it. Cheers.'

Chapter Three

Christy Kennedy was sitting on the longboat, sipping a cup of tea – one of his favourite occupations. Junior's recollection of the morning's events tallied pretty much with Martin's, excepting that he had not, it seemed, heard any splash.

Kennedy was thinking that he should make a trip on the boat himself to see if the noise of the engine was indeed loud enough to drown out a disturbance as loud as a body falling – or jumping – into the water. He was also considering asking for another cup of tea, when he recognised the voice of a new arrival. 'I know those tartan tones. Are you to be my bagman, Sergeant Irvine?' Kennedy asked the smartly-dressed detective walking down the tow-path towards him.

Detective Sergeant James Irvine straightened his bow tie before answering, 'Indeed I am, sir. Sorry to be a bit late. I've been otherwise engaged up on Primrose Hill all morning.'

'And what's been going on up there?'

'Some nutter was sniping at dogs from the high-rise flats. He killed four of the pets before we managed to disarm him.'

'What was ringing his bell, then?' Kennedy asked, not sure whether he should be amused or angry.

'Apparently, he was fed up going out for a walk on the hill every morning and ending up with dog-shit on his shoes.'

'Maybe it's the owners he should have been after, not the dogs. Anyway, can you put together a system for this? DC Milligan seems to have most of the facts at his fingertips. He'll fill you in. I'm going for a walk.'

Kennedy put his hands into his jacket pockets and wandered around the scene of the incident. He reminded himself that it was still the scene of an 'incident' and not yet the scene of a crime; perhaps that would come later. That was his job – to find out exactly what had happened.

Irvine's task would be to organise the whole shebang. By the time he'd arrived, the team was already in place. The first job was to seal off the area, using blue and white police tape. The photographer was busy snapping the corpse from as many angles as he could think of. When it looked like he was done, Irvine summoned the pathologist. 'All right, Dr Taylor, you're on.'

'A bit theatrical, old dear,' replied the good doctor.

'Just trying to make you feel at home, old bean. But don't get too comfortable, DI Kennedy will soon be over, wanting to know every last detail.'

As he carried his bag of tricks over to the corpse, Taylor muttered something about it not being an exact science but that he'd have a go. 'Good God!' he bellowed, as he knelt down beside the body.

Everyone on the scene turned to look – Irvine and Kennedy quickly made their way to his side. 'Something bothering you?' asked Kennedy, cool as ever.

'It's Eddie Berry!' whispered Taylor.

'You know him?' Irvine had a gift for asking the obvious.

'Good grief, yes.' The doctor searched for a breath that was failing him, and stood up to clear his head. He looked as if he was about to collapse. 'Just give me a moment, please.'

'Want some tea? Or something stronger?' asked Kennedy.

'Goodness, no – not while I'm on duty, Inspector. No, I'm okay, really. It was just such a shock. This man is a medical acquaintance of mine. Edmund Berry. He's a resident at St Pancras All Saints Hospital. Just give me a few seconds and I'll get on with it.'

Kennedy felt it best to leave Taylor to his own devices and inquired from Irvine if anything had yet been turned up by the uniformed lads.

'No, sir. Nothing out of the ordinary, just yet. But then – as ever – we don't know what we're looking for. But a bit of luck with Dr Taylor knowing the corpse.'

'I'm not sure he would agree with you. Let's keep on searching. Everything we need is out here waiting for us to find it.'

Kennedy contemplated the busy scene. Everyone was diligent in their own way and each alone with their thoughts. People would start to become talkative once the corpse was removed from the scene.

Taylor pulled on a pair of polythene gloves before commencing his examination of the corpse. His first mental note was that the body had not been in the water for long: a matter of hours. No blood or bruising was noticeable to the naked eye. He sealed the hands and feet in plastic bags and beckoned to Kennedy. 'I can't do much more till I get it down to the mortuary. Do you want to search the clothes before we remove the body?'

'Yes, I suppose I'd better.' Kennedy's reluctance must have been obvious as he called Irvine over to assist in the gruesome task.

Irvine and Kennedy knelt down on either side of the corpse before going through the pockets – the contents were placed in polythene bags. Kennedy was thankful that the eyes of the corpse were closed. In normal circumstances, the search would have helped to identify the body but, as Taylor had already solved that mystery, the collection of clues would hopefully shed light on Dr Berry's last hours.

'Not much here, sir,' concluded Sergeant Irvine. The search had produced a couple of pens – one a cheap Biro and the other a Parker – as well as a wallet stuffed with credit cards, receipts and various bits of paper which would be better examined once they'd had a chance to dry out. Irvine counted Berry's unspent money – two fifty-pound notes, seven twenty-pound notes, four ten-pound notes and a fiver – neatly folded in half and in ascending order.

Various coins were also extracted from Berry's pockets and Kennedy wondered if the deceased had had the same habit as himself of dumping his change into convenient large containers – every vase and bowl in his house and office was full of the stuff. He had never really worked out why he did it. Sometimes – for instance, early in the morning – it would be a pain to go into a newsagent with a ten-pound note for nothing more than the *Guardian*. When containers started overflowing with coins, he'd transfer the funds to a larger container with the intention of either bagging it for the bank or else dumping it in some charity collection box. Somehow, he never got round to doing either.

Kennedy noticed that Berry wore sensible shoes – expensive-looking but extremely functional. The job could make you something of an expert on shoes and the like and Kennedy deduced that this pair was no more than four or five years old and wearing well – the time in the water had not deadened the spit-and-polish shine. Berry's shoes were not unlike his own, and Kennedy wondered if he had purchased them from his own supplier – Ducker & Son of Oxford – but that would have been too much of a coincidence, he thought.

Irvine was examining a four-inch square of fawn material which he'd found in Berry's back pocket. 'Bit small for a handkerchief,' he muttered to no-one in particular.

'It's for cleaning his glasses,' answered Kennedy.

Sergeant Irvine was puzzled.

'Look at the two marks on the bridge of his nose. Look – there and there. He's a glasses man. And as spectacle-wearing people grow older, they become more fussy about keeping them clean – hence this little cloth. His specs may have came off when he hit the water. We might find them down below when the divers arrive.'

Kennedy brought the gruesome search to a conclusion. 'Nothing else of interest on the body. Have the wallet and its contents sent to my office when they've dried out, Sergeant. Now, do you think that location van has a brew going yet?'

Kennedy turned to Taylor. 'When you've… ah… sent the body on its way to the lab, will you join me for a cup of tea in the wagon and give me the SP on our corpse?'

After indicating his approval of Kennedy's suggestion, Taylor instructed the ambulance attendants to place the corpse in a body-bag and to deliver it to the mortuary at St Pancras All Saints Hospital.

As the ambulance – or meat wagon, as it was affectionately known – took Edmund Berry on his penultimate journey, Kennedy made his way back up the embankment, over the bridge to the main road and disappeared into the site wagon, a large, white mobile-office-on-wheels affair.

'That's that,' he said to himself sadly whilst he re-packed his box of mostly unused tricks. 'Now for that tea.'

Chapter Four

Dr Taylor found Kennedy up in the site wagon, drinking his tea and surveying the scene from on high. They had an extensive view of Cumberland Basin and the Feng Shang Boat Restaurant to the left of the cul-de-sac of the Regent's Canal.

Cumberland Basin is the point where the Regent's Canal, having run parallel to the zoo on one side and Prince Albert Road on the other, takes a left turn – assuming, that is, you're walking towards the basin. This left turns the canal in the direction of Camden Lock, the vibrant heart of Camden Town. The canal walk had recently become very popular, largely because of the multitude of colours, from the lively shades of the boats, through the numerous greens and browns of the trees, to the blue sky with puffy smoke-like clouds.

Kennedy was lost in his thoughts. Rather than disturb him, the doctor prepared his own cup of tea. The noise of the pouring tea soon caught Kennedy's attention and brought him back to the present with a jolt. 'I'll have a refill, Doctor – if there's another cup in the pot.'

'There certainly is,' replied Taylor generously. 'Pass me your cup.'

'Thanks. Milk and two sugars, please.'

The tea ritual completed, they sat at either end of an ugly mustard sofa, the site wagon's one attempt at comfort. But it was uncomfortably low , a matter of ten inches off the ground, and the other seating arrangements weren't much better, various chairs and swivel seats, all too high.

A couple of sips later, Kennedy became annoyed at the discomfort of the ridiculous sofa and dragged himself off, nearly spilling his precious tea in the process. He made his way back to the window. After contemplating the scene outside for a few moments, he quietly asked Taylor – whose large, generous frame was causing serious disturbance in the sofa – about the unfortunate Dr Berry. 'How long has he been dead, Doctor?

Kennedy was half-expecting the usual, Well, it's too early to tell but I'd say sometime within the last nine weeks – so he was more than surprised at Taylor's response. 'Well, judging by the degree to which the body has swollen, I'd say not too long – possibly three to six hours.'

'Hmm,' Kennedy replied, weighing up this information. 'And

would you say your colleague was still alive when he fell – or jumped or was pushed – into the water?'

'Quite possibly. But I won't know that until I open him up.'

Kennedy's stomach murmured a complaint at this statement. 'The timing is interesting, doctor,' began Kennedy, expelling from his mind the vision of the corpse being opened, 'because that would mean that the splash heard by our young friend may well have been that of Dr Berry's last swim, and so perhaps there was no foul play involved, perhaps it was just a simple suicide. There's no sign of a struggle, no obvious bruising to the body…'

'And I hear from young Milligan that no suicide note has yet turned up,' interjected Taylor.

'True enough, Doctor. I know it's not a popularly held belief that every suicide leaves a note but I think that in the majority of cases some message is left – written or not. Anyway, I put the horse before the cart. How about if you tell me all you know about Dr Berry,' suggested Kennedy.

'Well,' began Taylor, 'as I said earlier, I've known him a little socially over the last couple of years – since he came to work at St Pancras. He was gaining a strong reputation for his research into skin diseases. Seemed to be well-liked by his colleagues. He kept himself in good shape, as you can see, and he dressed well – as you no doubt also noticed.'

He paused to retrieve more information from his memory bank. 'Although we were both based at the same hospital, our departments are miles apart and we rarely bumped into each other. My contact with him has been mostly at friends' parties and I believe I can remember him telling me that he liked to play golf. Oh, yes – I believe he might have been a cricket fan, too. In fact, now I remember us having the usual cricket-fan conversation about how the best way to enjoy cricket was to simultaneously watch it on TV and listen to the commentary on Radio 3.'

'You didn't know him well enough, I suppose, to ascertain his state of mind?' asked Kennedy.

'No, I'm afraid not, Inspector. He seemed to have a fine sense of humour, but who knows? Who can tell what anyone is really thinking or feeling at a party – we all put on a show,' answered the doctor.

'What about his family?'

'Oh, God – I had forgotten… someone will have to tell his wife. Poor woman, and they had a son, I believe. A young family starting out with everything in front of them and then this. We sometimes forget the real victims, Inspector.'

Taylor's voice had gradually faded until it was almost inaudible. Snapping out of his moroseness, he decided to escape the sofa – an operation that proved complex and difficult. 'If you have no more questions, Inspector, I'll get back to the mortuary and see what else I can find out for you.'

'That's fine, Doctor. I'll speak to you later. Thanks a million,' Kennedy said quietly, as he rinsed the completely drained cup and returned it to the tea-making area.

Kennedy wandered around Cumberland Basin once more, looking down on the activity from the brim. The body had been removed and his eyes scoured the site over and over again, not sure what he was looking for. Just searching for something – anything that would explain the death of Dr Edmund Berry.

Chapter Five

WPC Anne Coles found herself mesmerised by Detective Inspector Kennedy's left hand as it continuously coiled and recoiled. They were on the doorstep of number 19 England's Lane. Kennedy rang the doorbell for a second time, then silently stepped a pace back whilst continuing to flex his hand. The exercise reminded WPC Coles of someone passing a two-pence piece through their fingers, but in her detective inspector's case, there was no coin – just the finger movement. The WPC stood five-foot-six-inches tall. She had blonde hair – natural – which had to be carefully orchestrated to fit within the confines of her regulation headgear. She wore little make-up on duty and much off duty.

The movement abruptly stops as a human sound was heard on the other side of the door – a female voice. 'No, it's not your Daddy – not yet. Go back to your toys, sweetheart.'

The door opened fully, revealing a stunningly beautiful woman.

'Mrs Berry?' inquired Kennedy with his quiet Irish lilt.

Kennedy noted how the woman's eyes acknowledged him as a stranger and how the twinkle was replaced by panic when she registered the WPC's uniform.

Kennedy is aware of what would be going on in her head at that moment. Her brain will be attempting to unscramble her confused thoughts. The police – something's wrong. It's like an internal damage assessment. Then the defences kick in. I can take all that you can tell me because this is not going to be the worst thing in my life. My son is safe behind me in my house and my husband is safe at work – so, how bad can it be? I can take it. All this flashes through her head in a split second, and she attempts to be cool and collected.

'Yes. What's wrong?' Her words stumble out, like unsuccessful punters emerging from the bookmaker's shop.

Mrs Berry's world had been fine until she opened the door to let the wickedness and the cold of the outside world into the warmth and safety of her home. Her life is about to be destroyed in a way she never thought possible.

'I'm Detective Inspector Christy Kennedy of Camden CID,' Kennedy flashed his ID, 'and this is WPC Anne Coles. Could we come in please, Mrs Berry?'

Mrs Berry is thinking – Okay, I'm in control – everything's fine. Probably some robbery and they're checking up. I can deal with that.

What will Edmund think when he finds out the police were in the house today? He'd know how to handle this.

'Yes, of course, do come in.'

Kennedy was thinking how it was impossible to prepare someone for the news he was about to give to this poor, unfortunate woman. You could, of course, try to make them comfortable – have them feel at ease – but then when you do it, when you tell them the news in your own pathetic way, it still knocks them off their feet.

Her eyes locked into Kennedy's the way a preyed animal uses an optic shield. She searched his face, his body movements, for some kind of clue. Seconds that seemed like hours were passing and she still didn't know why the police were here – in her house, her place of safety.

'I think you should sit down Mrs Berry and prepare yourself for a shock.'

She does so. How bad can this be?

'Has there been some kind of an accident, Inspector?'

'I'm afraid I have some bad news for you. A man we believe to be your husband has been found dead in the canal.' There – he'd said it. He'd managed to speak the words and the reaction – surprisingly – was rather calm.

'Ha! There must be some kind of mix-up, some kind of mistake. My husband is a doctor – he's at the hospital. He's on lates this week and is due back in a couple of hours. There's obviously been a terrible mistake – it can't be him.'

'I'm afraid it's very unlikely that there's been a mistake. A colleague of your husband has already informally identified the body. I'm sorry…'

A young boy runs into the room. Mrs Berry picks him up and holds him close to her – either to give or to receive comfort. Probably both. Perhaps, instinctively, to protect her sole remaining dependant. The boy reacts to his mother's infectious panic and starts to bawl with full force. This, in turn, intensifies his mother's fear. Mrs Berry suspends her disbelief and lets it all go.

It starts with a growl from deep inside of her and builds slowly. The animal-like whine the noise has become sounds not unlike the word 'No' – an evil sound, a sound that can be affected only by death, the wail of a banshee.

The longer the whine continues, the fiercer the son's sobs become. The son is too young to know exactly what is happening, but something beyond him – way beyond him – is controlling him. Instinct.

Kennedy stands still, a stranger in the house, observing – a spectator, not a participant. He feels helpless, impotent, feeble and incapable – but mostly helpless. The doctor's wretched wife – liquid streaming from her eyes and nose – has now totally broken down.

She nearly drops her son but the WPC is there in a flash and rescues him in her arms and tries to quieten and comfort him.

Kennedy signals the WPC with his eyes to take the son to another room, whilst he supports the wailing mother and guides her to the sofa. He holds her tight, trying to give her some of his warmth, his support, his strength, his pity. Her face is a mess and she accepts his offer of a bundle of tissues to attend to her nose and eyes. The flow of tears is uncontrollable. She is unable to catch her breath for long enough to say anything. Several times she tries to regain control of herself, to try to say something. But it's useless, the sobbing will not subside.

Kennedy feels his own eyes filling up. It was beyond sadness – it was emptiness. He forces himself to take stock of the room so as to divert his feelings and his thoughts.

The room has been carefully and lovingly put together with an obvious feminine touch. Two alcoves – one either side of the fireplace – are packed with books. Kennedy strains his eyes to try and pick out authors and titles – Peter Carey, Garrison Keillor, lots of Seamus Heaney and Larry McMurty.

Resting on the fireplace is a Dutch clock with family pictures on either side. In one, Dr Berry is showing off his wife and child to the camera. The son has definitely taken after his father – same rounded eyes – not unlike Paul McCartney, thinks Kennedy. These pictures of happiness will henceforth afford the viewers nothing but pain.

Mrs Berry takes deep breaths, trying to control the sobbing. She's trying to form words but still finds it impossible.

'I'm sorry.' It's all that Kennedy can find to say.

The doctor's wife again fights for words. Her main preoccupation now is thirst; her throat feels very, very dry. And she feels guilty for thinking such a mundane thought at that moment in her life.

'He'll never… he'll never be able to see what his son… what his son becomes… he really loved… he loved that boy…'

Again she is unable to control the tears.

Kennedy holds her tight once more. 'Is there anyone we could call – is there anyone you want with you?' Kennedy whispers as he rocks her back and forth.

No answer – more tears.

Just when he thinks she is finding some peace, she starts up again. It's beyond her control.

Some time later – it might have been minutes, it might have been hours – when the sobbing had subsided, she gathers all her strength and manages to utter, quietly and quickly, 'My sister… my sister, Doreen. Could you ring her please – the number's in the book by the phone – she'll come. Oh, God, I don't know what to do… how to handle this. What will I do? Sam – where's Sam?'

Assuming Sam is her son's name, Kennedy reassures her. 'He's with the WPC – Anne Coles. They're next door. Sam will be fine with Anne.'

Kennedy removes his arm from around Mrs Berry. 'I'll ring your sister and make you a strong cup of tea at the same time. Okay?'

'Inspector, how did it happen?'

Kennedy explains the approximate circumstances in which Dr Berry's body has been found, and concludes: 'We have to conduct tests to establish the exact cause of death.'

She nods. 'To think, he'll never see his son grow up…'

Chapter Six

Kennedy felt restless as he headed back to his office at North Bridge House. He hated these limbo periods, unable to proceed with the case until Dr Taylor's report arrived on his desk. If indeed there was a case at all. Perhaps Detective Constable Milligan's initial observation was correct, maybe it was a simple suicide after all. But from the little information he had gleaned, Kennedy doubted it. Dr Berry had a lot to live for: a successful career, an obviously caring wife, a son at an age when everything is new and exciting, an age when his adventures give as much joy to his parents as to himself.

The detective inspector turned on the old valve radio in his office – sometimes the cackle helped him to think. Not today. After a few minutes he made the radio silent again. Returning to his desk, he tried to involve himself in some paperwork but he couldn't progress beyond merely picking up a pen and holding it in his hand.

Kennedy's problem was that if there were suspicious circumstances in the case (and he certainly thought there were) then the longer he waited, the more difficult the case would be to solve. It was not unlike a long-distance race. In the early stages it didn't matter what your position was or how fast you ran, so long as you kept moving and in sight of the leaders. You always had a chance of catching up later, when the leaders had tired or drained themselves in their war of wills against each other. But the longer you stood still, as Kennedy felt he was doing just then, the further the leaders ran away from you and the harder they were to catch.

Then again, in a long-distance race, you at least knew which way you were supposed to be going. In the case of Dr Berry (if indeed there was to be a case of Dr Berry) he had no notion in the world of the direction he should be taking.

Kennedy was forced to admit that he was achieving little in the office, and so decided to walk the half-mile around the corner to Cumberland Basin and see how Detective Sergeant James Irvine and his team were progressing.

At the top of Parkway – on the junction with Prince Albert Road – stands a telephone kiosk. It is of the newer design, obviously copied from a small seaside guest house shower, and it had recently replaced the magnificent red box that Kennedy had such happy memories of. He thought fondly of the hours he had spent in such red sanctuaries. When still a schoolboy, he would talk to girlfriends for hours and then become truly sad when the money ran out – unless, of course, the girlfriend at the other end had a phone in her house and could ring him back. To him, telephone boxes, somewhere to take a girlfriend when it was raining, were very romantic places. You could turn down the light for a bit of privacy by screwing the bulb a few turns and Bob's your uncle. Mind you, if you did have an uncle called Bob, and he happened to see you canoodling with your friend, you were assured of a good clip on the ear. Because, by the time you returned home, Uncle Bob would have broadcast exactly what you had been doing and with whom. Here, Christy – what were you doing in the telephone box with old man Derby's daughter? Wallop!

The appearance of these new shower units annoyed Kennedy each and every time he passed them. They were hideous, unattractive, characterless – one of the ever-growing pimples on the London landscape. He slowed as he passed this particular eye-sore, debating whether or not to kick the glass in. Hardly the actions of a Detective Inspector, he admitted to himself as he pulled opened the door and entered the glass-walled booth. He inserted a ten-pence piece and dialled.

'Hello, *Camden News Journal*. How can I help you?' answered the voice, adopting the kind of tone you might use with a backward child.

'Could I have extension 1098, please?' replied Kennedy.

'Sorry, can you repeat it please? I didn't get the last number.'

'Usual problem, it's my accent,' Kennedy answered. 'Eight, 1098.' He said it slowly, with an emphasis on the eight, as in 'ate'.

'Putting you through.'

Kennedy was thanking somebody – probably God – that he didn't have to go through the usual indignity of, 'You know, eight – the one between seven and nine,' when his thoughts were interrupted by a woman's voice.

'Features.'

'Hi.'

'Christy, that you?' Her voice had quickly warmed from the official-sounding 'Features'.

'That's right. How'ya doing?'

'Great – you know, but busy. And you?'

The office voice was returning. He felt such a stupid man whenever he talked to this woman. 'Could we have a chat later?' he asked.

Telephonic silence for a time – seemingly too long a time to Kennedy and he was about to trot out the, 'It's okay – some other time, maybe,' line when she ended the silence in a distinctly non-office voice. 'Yes, Christy – that would be nice. See you in The Queens at eight. Okay?'

'Great, excellent. I'll leave you to it. Cheers.'

'See you later, Christy.'

Click, and she was gone.

He kept the phone in his hand, listening to the purr of the dialling tone for some seconds, before setting it back in its cradle.

'Bloody stupid boxes.' Kennedy spoke the words to no-one in particular, but British Telecom in general.

Chapter Seven

By the time Kennedy returned to Cumberland Basin, the team had come up with a big zero – absolutely nothing. Irvine was waiting for his okay to pack up and head back to the station.

'Right so, Jimmy – you can do your famous Rowdy Yates impersonation with the "pack 'em up and move 'em out" call.'

'Thank you, sir – although I'm not sure he would approve of the Sean Connery accent. But here we go.'

When Irvine had given the order to saddle up, Kennedy put another question to him. 'Where's the Sailing Diamond and our two chaps?'

'I let them go, sir, after we'd taken their statements. If they don't work they don't get paid.'

Kennedy nodded his assent and Irvine posed a question of his own. 'What do you think, sir? Suspicious circumstances or plain old suicide?'

Kennedy mused for a few moments.

'I don't know… there's nothing to be suspicious about, so that tends to make me suspicious. His wife is in a bad way so it'll be tomorrow before I can have a proper chat with her. But they seem to have been a very tight family. Oh, could you check out his financial position for me when you return to the station?'

'Yes, sir. What about his hospital? Should we start talking to the people up there?'

Again Kennedy considered his options.

'I think not. We should wait until we receive Taylor's report, which he's promised for first thing tomorrow morning. I'd like to wait till then before we start prodding around too much. I'd also like to try and find out how Berry got out here. Taxi? Bus? Car? Walked? Check with whoever was on duty in the hospital car-park. Find out where his car is. I'm assuming he has one somewhere.'

Irvine dutifully noted Kennedy's requirements as his boss extended the list. 'Check with the staff on the floating food parlour over there and visit the houses on the other side of the bridge. See can anyone remember a person fitting Berry's description around here late last night or early this morning. Have Milligan do the leg-work, he seems a bright lad.'

Irvine shook his ballpoint pen to give the ink a jolt.

'Oh, and tell Superintendent Castle where we're up to on this. I'll brief him in the morning once I've had a chance to appraise Dr Taylor's report. In the meantime, I think I'll wander back over to England's Lane and see how Mrs Berry and the WPC are getting on.' Irvine hardly looked up as Kennedy departed the scene. His attention was directed at his notebook, as he made a point-check to ensure he'd taken it all in.

Irvine admired Kennedy and he liked being 'bag-man' on Kennedy's cases. He found Kennedy easy to work with – never any tantrums. Kennedy believed in teamwork and always encouraged his team, not afraid of giving credit where credit was due, a pleasant change from some of the other senior detectives who would claim each and every successful idea as their own.

Being a Scotsman, Irvine appreciated Kennedy's dry sense of humour. Occasionally they had a drink together but by and large Kennedy seemed to prefer to keep himself to himself when not on duty. This need – but not preoccupation – for privacy was probably what had earned Kennedy his 'dark horse' reputation around the station.

Good luck to him, Irvine thought. He much preferred that attitude to the 'let's get our hands dirty and muck in with the peasants' approach of some of the other, more career-conscious senior officers.

Chapter Eight

They could just as easily have missed each other, thought Kennedy. It was about ninety minutes after he had left DS Irvine and he was sipping a cool glass of white wine in The Queens at the foot of Primrose Hill.

On his way over, he had stopped off at the Berry home in England's Lane to find that the sister, Doreen Clarke, had taken charge of the household. Sheila Berry was in bed, sedated and trying to gain comfort in deep sleep. Her son, Sam, and WPC Coles were playing, and for the time being he was content with his cars, years away from feeling the full impact of the loss of his father.

Kennedy hung around for about an hour, chatting with Doreen. He promised to return in the morning when he would talk with Sheila.

He had half an hour to kill and decided not to eat in case dinner was on the cards, so that was how he found himself sitting in The Queens, sipping wine, thinking about their first meeting. It had been at Heathrow Airport. Kennedy had been aware of her three times in a matter of two days. Which was opportune because his mother used to say that he should not talk to a woman until he had met her three times and had been formally introduced.

The first occasion had been in the book department of W. H. Smith's, in the departures area. He thought immediately that she was stunning, and as far as Kennedy could tell, she was wearing no make-up. Short, black hair, but not boyish short, more like a Beatle-cut from the era of *A Hard Day's Night*. She wore a quiet black suit with a white shirt and carried an overcoat over one arm. Her other hand held a book and she periodically pushed a brown leather shoulder bag back into position so that she could browse . He couldn't quite make out the title; he squinted in a wasted effort to identify the book but quickly gave up in case anyone thought he was staring.

Kennedy walked to the other end of the bookshop to position himself for a better look at her. She had such gorgeous eyes which broke into a wonderful, brief smile whenever someone excused themselves to pick up a book she was blocking.

He sometimes felt that this was the only way for true love. You see someone for a glimpse, a split second, and their body-power over-comes you to a point of total distraction. In that second, you find true love. You have no arguments, no fights, no jealousies, no guilts, no sorrows, no games, no hate: that love is perfection. It's only when you have to deal with the weakness of human nature that it starts to crumble.

The second time was when their eyes locked in the arrivals hall at Dublin Airport. Again, a second – a split second – and she was gone. But that hint of a smile burned into his mind's eye.

The third time was when she took the seat next to him on the return flight the following day. Technically this was the third time, although he was not sure such a statement would hold up in court. But once they were both seated comfortably, he formally introduced himself. He was not altogether certain this was what his mother had meant but desperate times called for desperate measures.

Kennedy always felt awkward on these occasions but there was something about her that gave him the confidence to try and make the connection.

'I saw you in the bookstore yesterday at Heathrow – did you find anything worth buying?' Well, it was a start.

'No,' she half-laughed. 'I don't know why I browse in airport bookstores, I rarely find anything I want to read.'

He didn't know what else to say; it was one of those occasions when you're so busy trying to think of something that won't sound stupid that you end up wordless.

She seemed at her ease. 'It's just that I have this problem walking past bookstores, I love them. I could, and do, spend hours in them.'

'Same here. And at airports it at least kills time,' he replied, not even thinking of what he was saying. It seemed a suitable moment to introduce himself. 'I'm… erm… Christy Kennedy.'

He offered his hand.

'I'm ann rea,' she answered.

They shook hands.

'I know that name. Yes – small a, small r. You write for *Camden News Journal*, don't you?'

'That's right.'

And the smile in her eyes lit up Kennedy's heart. Kennedy could picture it now, as he waited for her in The Queens.

They had talked about her work, and she explained the lower-case business. 'If I'm honest, it's probably to gain attention. I got the idea from kd lang. Apparently, she nicked it from e e cummings.'

They talked about music, their likes and dislikes. Up to that point, Kennedy had never heard of kd lang. He had since listened to, and been inspired by, 'Crying', a duet kd had performed with Roy Orbison.

The flight and conversation ended at about the same time. Kennedy really wanted to find a way to continue, to make the connection. He couldn't find a convenient way to do so. ann rea had been friendly and jovial, to a point. Kennedy thought she was comfortable communicating with strangers, totally at her ease. He didn't want to appear to hassle her so he left her packing her gear on the plane with a quiet, 'Nice to meet you. Goodbye.'

The Queens was filling up. He looked at his watch – seven forty-five. It would be another fifteen minutes before he saw ann rea again.

Following the plane journey, their next meeting had been six weeks later, in The Queens. Kennedy had been sharing a rare drink with DS Irvine. He enjoyed these occasions with Irvine, who didn't need to consume vast quantities of alcohol to be entertaining company. The detective sergeant had hundreds of stories and an amusing delivery.

'So, did you listen to kd lang yet?' the voice had enquired from behind him.

Kennedy didn't require visual confirmation – he knew immediately that it was ann rea. He turned and smiled his rare smile. 'Yes, I did, actually. I love her duet with Roy Orbison – what's the song called… "Crying". Yes, that's it, "Crying".'

He offered her his hand to shake. She took it but used it to pull him towards her to kiss him on the cheek. This kiss warmed his soul and he became embarrassed as he felt a flush rise in his cheeks. 'I'm sorry,' he said, 'this is my colleague, James Irvine.' Irvine and ann rea shook hands.

'What are you doing in The Queens? A bit off your path isn't it?' Kennedy enquired.

'I'm doing an interview in the studios in Mayfair Mews – just along the street a bit. You know what it's like ,any sign of a break in the work and they all pile down to the pub. But they seem to be going back now so I'd better leave, too,' smiled ann rea.

'Ah,' was all Kennedy could manage.

'Good to see you again, Christy.'

By now, Kennedy liked ann rea; he liked her a lot. He found himself thinking about her more and more and longed for their next chance meeting. When that didn't happen, he took the plunge and rang her to invite her out for dinner.

ann rea made Kennedy feel comfortable and at ease, but always excited, even when he really wanted to be nervous. The next time, it was she who contacted Kennedy and again they went to dinner. Since then, they'd been out together several times and were in the process of becoming good friends.

Kennedy wished for more but didn't want to rush it. There seemed to be no other men in her life and in the meantime, they enjoyed each other's company.

Kennedy was brought back to the present by the third chime of eight resounding from the pub clock, just as ann rea made her entrance. They greeted each other with a peck on the cheek.

'The usual, ann rea?'

'Yes please. I'm dying for one; could you fetch me a Ballygowan as well. I don't want to quench my thirst with wine. Ta, Christy.'

The landlady – the colourful Mrs Emily Tilsey – served Kennedy. 'Two dry white wines and a Ballygowan please, Mrs T. How's Hugh – don't see him around tonight?'

'He's fine. Pigeon night tonight – best place for him,' she said as she poured the two glasses of wine. 'Keeps him out from under my feet. That'll be three-twenty, Christy.'

Carrying the two wines in one hand and the Ballygowan in the other, he returned to ann rea. She did take his breath away – clichés were only clichés because sometimes they were true. He treasured her company. At this point in their relationship they supposedly didn't mean a lot to each other so he was always very careful not to be too forward with his affections.

ann rea had obviously just spent a day working hard, but she glowed rather than wilted. He asked himself, How was it they had met at this point in their lives? How come one so special was not already spoken for? These thoughts filled his head as he sat down beside her. He would have been completely happy just to stare at her and listen to her. He didn't want to appear to be a complete idiot so he decided he'd better say something – anything – but before he got a chance, she spoke first.

'Are you okay? You sounded so low and so sad when you rang today.'

'Ah yes,' began Kennedy, remembering the events of the day. 'We fished this poor sod out of the canal this morning, over at Cumberland Basin. It looks like – but doesn't feel like – a simple suicide, and I'd just been to break the news to his widow. I still can't get used to that part of the work, no matter how many times I do it.'

He searched for the right words.

'I can never do it well, I can't easily deal with death. I know you're meant to be detached and unemotional about it but when you inform the relatives and you see the mental explosion taking place… ah, there are no words for it. But no matter how bad I feel, I know that her pain is a million times worse and that nothing – absolutely nothing – can be done to help her. There's no escaping that pain, there's no way round it. She just has to go through it herself, the poor woman.'

They sat in their own silence for a few minutes.

Chapter Nine

The following morning, Kennedy awoke with his usual hunger for the day. He hoped it would be more productive than the one before – in more ways than one.

The first three items on his agenda would hopefully ascertain how Dr Berry died, whether by his own devices or through foul play. These thoughts filled his mind as he made his way briskly over Primrose Hill and down towards Camden Town.

The morning was sharp – he could see his breath before him, but at least it was dry. Kennedy never tired of the beauty of Primrose Hill, particularly on such early morning walks. The sky was a powerful blue and the green and brown colours of the hill combined to create his personal living picture-postcard. He felt very privileged to live where he did.

Seagulls croaked noisily overhead. Stormy at sea, he thought. His normal route to the office took him past Cumberland Basin. This morning, there were no signs whatsoever that twenty-four hours earlier, a man had lost (or maybe taken) his life there. The show goes on with or without you. He reached North Bridge House at his regular time of seven-forty-five, but instead of entering the Camden CID building, he turned left and headed down Parkway.

Parkway bridges the neo-classic elegance of Prince Albert Road (Regent's Park) with the vibrant High Street (Camden Town). The buildings are less sober, and more colourful, the further down Parkway you travel. From the top of the road – the traffic lights outside the disused York and Albany pub – to the bottom – the traffic lights just before Camden Town tube station – you have a police station, a record company, six pubs, nine estate agents, two dry cleaners, a launderette, an off-licence, a late night club (the famous Jazz Café), a cinema, and a pet shop.

Not to mention three hairdressers, two sportswear shops, one optometrist, a post office, a deli, a camera shop, one travel agent, a photo-studio with picture framers included and a toy shop – don't forget the toy shop. A hobby store, a tile shop, one gents clothes store, a locksmith and a garage.

And there's a vacuum cleaner service centre, and talking about centres, there's the Camden Career Centre and then there's the *International Wrist Watch Magazine* headquarters, four Camden-type clothes shops, an art gallery, a florist, a photocopying and print shop, and a mysterious temple of hipness whose contents are unusable, unwearable and unaffordable.

One bank, three newsagents – well, two-and-a-half really – the one at the top of the Parkway is seldom open and on the rare occasion he is open for business in the afternoon, he's sold out of papers but he does a great line in ladies tights. Two sandwich shops, one bookie, one council centre for the homeless, one dole office, eleven office buildings, one concert ticket box office, two ugly parking-ticket machines, ten trees, a billboard site, one telephone kiosk, one double telephone unit open to the elements, eleven streetlights, three sets of traffic lights and one of the best bookstores in London. What more could a man, woman or policeperson ask for?

Oh yes, and we mustn't forget the fourteen eating establishments, which count among their number The Salt and Pepper, Kennedy's favourite café and his destination that particular morning.

'The usual, guv?' inquired the jovial proprietor.

'Yes, please,' Kennedy smiled.

'Here or to go?'

'Actually, I think I'll take it here this morning, boss.'

Kennedy made his way past the service counter into the comfortable seated area in the back, finding the corner seat – his favourite – available and waiting.

Kennedy often popped into The Salt and Pepper for a cup of tea and a chat with witnesses, suspects, colleagues or friends. He actually had few friends, as he preferred just a few trusted people rather than a large group who couldn't be anything more than acquaintances.

Michael, the owner of The Salt and Pepper, made demon bacon sandwiches, semi-crisp with the fat removed and very hot in brown bread.

Two rounds of the very same, along with a steaming hot cup of tea (two sugars and a good dollop of milk), were now placed in front of Kennedy and he was ready to tuck in. First he removed the envelope which had been dropped through his letter-box earlier that morning.

The letter was from ann rea and it was the first letter that she had written to him. Actually, it was more of a note, but you had to be thankful for small mercies.

Enclosed, the couple of features on Dr Berry I was telling you about. Hope they're of use. You owe me a drink!

Talk to you later.

ann rea

He had already read the note earlier. Written with a fountain pen, the handwriting was smooth. No 'regards', 'cheers' or 'love' before her name. He considered this for a time as he stared at the note.

'She must have been up early,' he said quietly to the cup of tea he raised to his lips. He reckoned ann rea must have gone into her office at dawn, found the articles, photocopied them and driven around to deliver them. What a woman.

He took some comfort that, for ann rea to go to all that trouble, she must have some goodwill for him. 'A little, perhaps,' he said to himself as he tucked into the sandwiches.

Munching happily, Kennedy read the first of the articles.

STRANGE DEATH OF LOCAL TEACHER

Local teacher, Susanne Collins of Primrose Hill Primary School, died late Friday – 22nd January – in St Pancras All Saints Hospital. Ms Collins (28), who lived in Camden Town, had taught at Primrose Hill Primary School for five years. She was admitted to the hospital on Wednesday 20th January at lunchtime for what was described as 'routine treatment for a common ailment.'

Underneath the single-column article was a photo of a smiling, vibrant Ms Collins. But why was it included? There was no mention of Dr Berry. Kennedy took a large swig of tea and read on. He soon had his answer. The larger article, again accompanied by the same picture, was dated a week later, the *Camden News Journal* being a weekly newspaper.

MYSTERY DEEPENS IN 'PRIME-OF-LIFE TEACHER' DEATH

Mystery surrounds the circumstances under which much-loved local teacher, Ms Susanne Collins (28) died at St Pancras All Saints Hospital on Friday 22nd January. Ms Collins was a popular teacher at Primrose Hill Primary School.

Ms Collins was supervising the children in the playground on Wednesday lunchtime when witnesses report that her legs buckled from under her and she fell to the ground. She was taken immediately to St Pancras All Saints Hospital, where she was placed under observation.

Two days later, her condition deteriorated and she was rushed to the operating theatre where she died during an operation to treat a blood clot. Dr Edmund Berry, the senior hospital doctor treating her, issued the following statement on behalf of the Hospital Trust:

'It is too early to say what happened. We are carrying out a full investigation into the matter and will make public our findings at the earliest opportunity.'

William Jackson, Ms Collins' boyfriend and teaching colleague, was said to be 'devastated'. A friend said, 'We just can't believe it. One day she's seemingly in perfect health, then she's admitted to hospital and, two days later, she's dead.'

Ms Susanne Collins is survived by her father, Mr Tom Collins and a brother, Mr Norman Collins, who live at the family home in Derby.

End of article.

End of story?

Although it was slim pickings, Kennedy decided that he'd check on any further developments when he visited the hospital later to interview Dr Berry's colleagues about his own demise. But if those two cuttings were all the *Camden News Journal* had on him, Dr Berry couldn't have led a very wayward existence. But there again, it's usually the quiet ones...

He washed down the last bite of the bacon sandwich with the final mouthful of tea – perfect when both food and drink run out simultaneously. Kennedy paid the bill and walked back up Parkway to his office at North Bridge House. He was intrigued as to what information the autopsy of Dr Berry would now offer up.

Chapter Ten

North Bridge House was built on the site of the very first settlement in Camden. It was originally a monastery in the days when the monks tended their pigs up on Primrose Hill. Through the years, it had successfully served several purposes before becoming the home of the then newly formed Camden CID, in 1967. Prior to that, it had been a private school and Kennedy had often felt he'd inherited the headmaster's study.

As he entered his office, Kennedy switched on his valve radio and after a short delay, Capital Gold came through loud and clear. It was either that, Radio 4 or GLR, depending on Kennedy's needs and his moods. He always thought of his office more as a thinking room, and it was very homely, especially by police standards. Bit by bit, Kennedy had very quietly replaced the standard police furniture with snug pieces he'd found in Camden's second-hand shops. It really was surprising what you could pick up for next to nothing.

Kennedy didn't mind the time and elbow-grease he expended doing up the bits of furniture. His dad was a carpenter and he had learnt a few tricks of the trade while growing up. He was usually working on some piece or other – a chair, a table, a desk, a wooden ornament – anything, just as long as there was something there to work with. He found it extremely therapeutic, and a great way to focus the mind. He loved the aroma of wood shavings, glue, varnish, paints, missing only the smell of his father's sweat from childhood. Kennedy remembered fondly the hours he had spent with his dad in his workshop. His father would patiently answer his numerous questions, some about the job in hand, others about the worries of life. Many of the realities he had learnt from his father in those long-gone days had stood him in good stead since.

The ambience the furniture created in his office was helped by the fact that all the walls were panelled with a rich walnut wood. Kennedy could hardly believe that in some of the other offices they had stripped the wood from the walls or slapped a coat of paint over the top. To the amusement of his colleagues, Kennedy had spent a great deal of time restoring the wood in his room. He felt his father would be proud of him. Funny, that no matter what age you are – from six to sixty – you feel the need to impress your parents.

The wall behind his desk supported the usual noticeboard with memos, schedules, rosters, awards, promotions, even a few wanted posters. To the left of his desk was another noticeboard, for his case-in-progress notes. It was old, covered in green felt with a large Guinness is Good for You logo carved into the frame. Here, Kennedy pinned all the details, photographs, clues, hunches, maps and sometimes even bluffs, in case his superior – Superintendent Castle – wanted to check up on his work while he was out.

While engrossed in a case, Kennedy had a habit of swinging his forties-style wooden swivel chair slightly to the left, tilting back, and resting his feet on the corner of the desk, while cogitating the contents of his case-board.

He removed the remnants of his previous case, and placed them in a box marked with the case title. Kennedy was a collector-creature and could not bear to throw anything away. He wondered aloud what the current case would become known as. Or would it, in fact, fit DC Ian Milligan's 'simple suicide' theory? There was no-one to answer his question because there was no-one to hear it.

Dr Taylor knocked on Kennedy's office door, disturbing his thoughts.

'Ah, do come in. You're early. Join me for a cup of tea? I've a pot brewing.'

'Yes – oh, yes please,' the doctor replied. Kennedy was the only senior police officer the doctor knew who made his own tea, and very palatable it was, too.

Both men settled comfortably into their seats and sipped their tea. Kennedy spoke first: 'Well, Doctor, what do you have for me?'

'Dr Berry died by drowning – pure and simple drowning. Water in his lungs. I would say that by the lack of swelling of the body and by its slight discolouration, he would have drowned sometime between 7am and 8am yesterday morning. It's hard to be more accurate due to the fact that the low temperature of the canal water would have reduced the body temperature quicker than normal. The alcohol level in his blood was high – as in, very high. Our Dr Berry had consumed vast amounts of spirits in his last few hours alive. I would go so far as to say a dangerous amount of spirits.'

'Hmm,' said Kennedy, interrupting for the first time.

When Taylor was convinced that Kennedy had no other observations to add, he continued: 'Berry's last meal would have been around six o'clock the previous night. He ate a good full meal: steak, potatoes – still in their skins – peas, carrots and green beans. I'd say he liked brown sauce with his steak.'

'How on earth do you know all that?' smiled Kennedy.

'The contents of his stomach – he didn't have time to digest his food properly.' Now it was Taylor's turn to smile – all experts enjoy their 'magic tricks', where their particular science affords them knowledge which could be amusing or enlightening to the layman.

'One other thing worth mentioning, Detective Inspector,' the doctor continued, consulting his notes. 'Dr Berry had a contusion under his arms which ran across the front of his chest. It may have been caused when they pulled him out of the water. The hooks could have pulled his clothes up under his arms and left a mark from the weight of his body.'

'No other contusions to report?' queried Kennedy.

'Nothing else. He was essentially in perfect health,' Taylor concluded, ruling out one possible reason for suicide.

Chapter Eleven

Kennedy was pinning sheets of paper to his noticeboard. *Edmund Berry. Drowned. Very drunk. Chest marked. 7–8am. Cumberland Basin.*

After staring at the sheets of paper, he buzzed WPC Anne Coles on the intercom, and asked her to be his driver for the morning.

Kennedy rode up front in the car with the WPC, unusual for a detective inspector. He seemed disturbed by the peacefulness of Primrose Hill as they drove past it on their way to the Berry residence on England's Lane.

WPC Coles did not have a chance to share Kennedy's thoughts, as he remained quiet until they reached the house. His fingers were agitated again as she rang the doorbell for the second time in twenty-four hours.

Doreen Clarke opened the door and immediately invited them into the house. Outside, the sky was overcast with darkening clouds. Inside, it felt as though the sun had gone down forever. Either Doreen had lost her battle to keep her sister's ebbing spirits afloat or else, and perhaps just as likely, she too was feeling the loss of an important and vital life.

The two adults in the house were obviously doing their best to conceal their heartaches from Sam, who was getting on with his life of innocence. Kennedy wondered what memories of his father he would treasure and carry in his subconscious to later life. Would those memories curse him, strengthen him, help him, hinder him or preoccupy him? Kennedy supposed it would all depend on the strength, love and stability his mother could give to him over the coming years.

He wondered would she dedicate her life entirely to her son, which would probably be wrong for both of them, or would she, after a time, also pick up the pieces of her own life and find another man? He was equally sure that these were the last thoughts in her mind at this moment.

Kennedy spoke to Doreen. 'How is she today?' His voice, in its usual quietness, seemed to suit the atmosphere of the house perfectly.

'Up and down, Inspector.'

Kennedy gently interrupted her. 'Call me Christy, please.' He felt that formalities were definitely out of place on such an occasion.

Doreen continued. 'She'll be just about to lift her spirits and then a word, or a sentence, or a thought, will remind her of him. She'll realise what has happened and start crying again. She'll be talking to you and will say something about Eddie and you can see in her eyes that she's doing a "fast-forward", realising he's dead – and then she'll lose it completely. I just don't know what to do, Inspector, er... Christy,' Doreen sighed.

WPC Coles was touched by Kennedy's comforting presence. He didn't need to say much – it was his air, his body language – very supportive, very strong, non-threatening. She felt that either the DI was very used to dealing with these situations or he was feeling somewhat hurt inside himself.

'Just being here is enough for her at this point, Doreen. There really is nothing else anyone can do to help. There is no help. But the fact that you are here for her and for her son is more important than you will ever imagine. You have to keep your energy and strength up. She'll cling to your strength. That strength and the passage of time will pull her through this.'

'I know, I'm sorry Insp– Christy. I just want to help, you know? But I feel so... so helpless,' she replied, yet she seemed to have taken strength from Kennedy's words and was soon inquiring would either of them like a cup of tea.

'Now you're talking!' said Kennedy, rubbing his hands together in a bid to lighten things up a little. As Doreen made her way to the kitchen he followed asking, 'Do you think that Sheila will feel up to talking to me later?'

'I think so, sir... er, Christy.' She found it difficult to address a policeman by his Christian name. 'She was saying earlier that she wanted to find out exactly what had happened. I think she hopes it will help her come to terms with Eddie's death.'

A few minutes later the tea was ready.

'Shall I set the table?' Doreen inquired.

'No, no – not at all,' he smiled. 'Just a wee cup of tea in our hands.'

'What?' Doreen seemed puzzled.

'Sorry. It just reminded me of when I was growing up. My mother would have two levels of tea-making. The very formal level when people came to visit and when we'd have the full works – tea, sandwiches, cakes, buns – all set up at the table and we would switch off the TV. The other level was when friends would just casually drop in for a chat or whatever and my mother would say, "Fancy a wee cup of tea in your hands?" I always had an image of my dad, who was a bit of a joker, coming into the living-room with the teapot and doing just that – pouring the tea into people's cupped hands.'

They laughed and he sat Doreen down at the table and poured her some tea – in the cup of course – and brought a cup for the WPC into the living-room. He found Sam trying to explain to the constable the need for the driver to go into his toy car upside down.

'Obviously an Australian driver,' Kennedy said to them both and then mouthed to Coles, 'I'm going to have a chat with Doreen in the kitchen,' before making his exit in that direction.

'Tell me all you can about Dr Berry, please?' he asked, as he sat down opposite her at the table.

'Well, let me see… what can I say?'

And she thought for some time.

Kennedy realised his question was too general so he asked another to help start her up.

'How did Sheila and Edmund meet?'

She smiled – a smile of memories – and Kennedy could see her eyes going to another time, another place.

'Actually,' she began after a few more silent moments, 'Sheila and I were out together the first time they met. We were shopping in Liberty's in Regent Street. We were looking for a birthday present for our father. They have some real "off the wall" presents in Liberty's and we've never failed to find Christmas and birthday presents for our parents there. It's a kind of ritual. We've been doing it for about twelve years and we're never let down.

'Anyway, we were in the basement – I think it was the basement – yes, the basement, because we were about to visit the coffee shop, and Eddie was there as well and they bumped into each other. Their eyes met and I could tell something special had happened. You know, you grow up romanticising about love at first sight and dreaming about it. It was weird being there; witnessing it, being a spectator. They were both powerless to do anything about it. It had happened – they had met, they had not spoken a word and I was the one being made to feel the stranger.

'So eventually, they spoke – well, actually he spoke to me first, though all the time never taking his eyes off Sheila. He asked us who we were – he was very friendly for a stranger. He had a very heartening way of talking to you. It was a natural charm but not a performance, if you know what I mean.'

Doreen blushed slightly at this point as she realised that Kennedy shared similar qualities.

'He asked us both to join him for a coffee in the Liberty's coffee shop and within twenty minutes they were talking away as if they had known each other all their lives. They went out to dinner that night – "Of course, you must come as well," he had said to me, but a gooseberry I am not. They dated heavily for the next few weeks. She moved into his house within a month and they married six months later.'

Kennedy smiled warmly.

'Sheila and Eddie were deeply in love, Christy; probably from the first moment they met in Liberty's. When Sam was born a year after they mere married, their lives were complete – yes, complete,' Doreen concluded, happy to savour that thought for a few moments.

Kennedy honoured this space and he contentedly sipped at his tea for sometime before continuing. 'How did they do financially?'

Doreen regrouped her thoughts. 'Quite well, actually. Not stinking rich, but they didn't have to struggle. Sheila is a partner in a PR firm. It's small but it does exceedingly well. She had saved quite a bit before they married and after the wedding Eddie sold his house and they bought this place together. They bought it very cheap but spent a lot of money – and even more love – doing it up into the way it is now.' She waved her hand around the kitchen.

'A grand home,' Kennedy said.

'They seemed fine. A car each. Sheila never complained about a cash shortage. In fact, she was always asking me if I was all right, was there anything I needed?'

'Hmm.' Kennedy considered his next question. 'Any other problem you were aware of?'

'No. None at all. We're particularly close and I'm positive she'd got her act together, as they say. In fact, she had her act together in a big way. I certainly admired her.' After some consideration, Doreen added, 'Both of them, in fact. The three of us, apart from being related, were great mates. We had some great times together... and now this.'

'What about drink? Did Dr Berry drink a lot?'

'He liked a little red wine now and again – with a meal or on a special occasion. But I've never seen him under the influence and Sheila said that he never overdid it. Her last boyfriend was a sober angel and a drunk devil and she commented on the difference when she started to go out with Eddie. He liked to keep in shape for his work.'

'No spirits?'

'I don't think so. I think he drank mineral water at parties and receptions but you should check with Sheila when you chat with her.'

'Yes, okay. Perhaps I should do that now. Do you want to see if she's up to it or not?'

Chapter Twelve

Kennedy was on his third cup of tea. He was about to talk to Sheila Berry, his second interview of the day. You would have been forgiven for thinking that it was Mrs Berry – not Kennedy – who was the stranger in the house that morning, given the way he sat her down at the table, making her feel comfortable and fetching her a cup of tea.

He noticed how hard she was trying to keep it together. It was obvious she wanted to appear as near normal as possible for the benefit of the child.

'Do you know yet what happened to Eddie, Inspector?'

Kennedy sipped at his tea, paused for some moments, and then sipped some more tea, using the space to ascertain how much she was capable of taking in. He sensed that the person sitting before him at the dining-table was not a weak, defenceless widow, but a very strong mother out to protect and take care of her only child. She was fulfilling one of the basic laws of the jungle.

'Well,' he began, 'as far as we can gather, sometime early yesterday morning – between the hours of seven and eight o'clock, he came to be in the Regent's Canal at the Cumberland Basin. He drowned. There are no suspicious circumstances, no evidence of foul play.'

He paused to see how she was taking this in and carefully proceeded. 'He had a great deal of alcohol in his body at the time of his death.'

'But that's impossible, he hardly drank. When he did, it was just a little red wine and he was always with me,' she blurted out.

He could see the look of shock and horror in her kind face, as she came to some realisation.

'Oh, God! Oh, no! You don't think he became drunk so that he could jump into the canal and take his own life do you? Oh no, it's not possible... it's just not possible. He'd never, ever do that. He loved Sam so much, you should have seen them together, here, here at this table.'

The table was large and cluttered with newspapers, toys, keys, books, timetables, leaflets, a small television, a radio with the façade of a jukebox, a bowl of spare change, Game Boy, and photos. It was obviously the main family meeting-cum-talking, eating, drinking and playing point. It was old and sturdy and the centre point of the kitchen.

'Eddie was so proud of his son – we both were very proud of Sam and spent hours upon hours planning his future.'

She paused for a moment.

'He rarely drank, and never just for the sake of drinking. Always with a meal and always with me. I've seen him tipsy or merry a few times but never drunk.'

Kennedy was quick to reassure her. 'Doreen told me the same thing.' He was particularly anxious to ensure that she didn't slip into the 'He's the police so he won't believe a word I say' routine.

'But then,' she began, a new panic overtaking her, 'if he didn't fall in the canal, that would mean…' The rest of the sentence went unspoken.

Again Kennedy jumped in. 'Well, that's what I have to do. I have to find out exactly what happened.' As an afterthought, he added, 'And that's what you are helping me to do.'

They both remained silent, neither knew how long, both brains racing ahead with different story lines. Sam came into the kitchen and climbed up on his mother's knee. After some minutes, she told him to go back into the living-room and play with Auntie Doreen because she and the kind policeman had some more chatting to do.

'I can leave this to later,' he offered.

'No – I'm fine, really. I would prefer to do this now. If I keep my brain active on your questions I can keep from thinking bad thoughts. I have to be strong. I have to, for Sam's sake.'

She physically composed herself before continuing.

'Really, Inspector – I'm fine to go on… I want to go on. What else do you want to know?'

'Well, okay – if you're sure now, but if at anytime you want to stop, just…'

She nodded.

'Your husband – did he walk a lot?'

Mrs Berry was bemused. 'Not particularly – why?' she asked.

'No particular reason – just background. Did he have a sweet tooth?'

She smiled.

He was surprised how much her face lit up with the smile. Not in the same way that ann rea's smiling eyes lit up her face and certainly in a much less sensuous way. He briefly remembered the carefree look Mrs Berry had displayed when she had opened the door to him the previous day.

'Yes, he did,' she answered. 'I don't know who was worse – Eddie or Sam. Eddie loved those chocolate-centred peanuts and Twirl bars. He loved Twirl cold, so I always kept the fridge stocked up for him, with a few spares hidden for an emergency. But what a funny question.'

Kennedy was trying to keep it light. He was trying to keep her out of that deep darkness she would unquestionably fall back into. 'How long did it take you to do this place up? It's really brilliant,' he said.

'Oh, probably three years on and off. When we first got together we talked about things and we realised that we both shared an ambition of finding a home and really making it our own, to do everything exactly as we needed and loved. When we bought the place it was a real mess and we got it dirt cheap – that way, we could afford to spend lots of money doing it out the way we wanted. We did this room first before we moved in. When we did move in, we practically lived in here for the first year or so, which is why this room seems to have become and remained the focus of the house. I'll leave Sam in the living-room to come out here to start dinner or something and I'll turn around a few minutes later and he'll be sitting at this table playing away. I was surprised that Eddie, being a doctor, was so good with his hands. I'm useless, although I landed all the painting jobs. He kept referring to me as the "paid distraction". I love this house, you know, but it does seem so empty without him.'

'Did anyone from the hospital help you with the work here?'

But she was still lost in her last thought.

'Sorry – what did you say?'

'Did anyone from the hospital help you do the work on the house?'

'We did it all by ourselves – well, along with help from this great Irish builder-cum-carpenter. Ossie Flynn was his name. He was great fun and he'd walk around saying all these great Irishisms. "So, it's yourself, is it?" "You'll never be half the man your mother was." Eddie and I would be in stitches laughing and Ossie would be wondering what we found amusing. Ossie helped Eddie with the heavier work – he was brilliant and could turn his hand to anything. But Eddie wanted to do most of the work himself. It was a labour of love and, as I've said, an ambition we both shared. We kept talking about it – planning the various rooms – even before we found the house. Part of me thought both of us were mad and that when the time came we would both chicken out. But no – he was as good as his word. Mostly it was hard work but we had some good fun, too.' She smiled at the memory of their secret shared antics.

'Was he ambitious at the hospital – in his work, I mean?' Kennedy inquired.

'Well, he was and he wasn't, if you know what I mean.'

Kennedy raised his eyebrows questioningly.

'Well, yes, I suppose – he really wanted to do well at medicine and make progress with his career. But he was in no great hurry. He always used to say that the only way to become a great doctor was to be an older doctor. He felt there were no short cuts to experience and he was happy to bide his time until his moment came. He was very conscious about Sam growing up and we talked about that a lot – about not allowing Sam to grow up with his father out at work all the time. Perhaps you've heard the medical joke – I was ten years old before I realised my father's first name wasn't Doctor.'

Kennedy laughed, although the sound of laughter felt alien in this house.

Sheila continued, unaware of his awkwardness. 'He wanted to be a father and a husband in attendance. He wanted to be a doctor and he wanted to be great at all three and he was prepared to work hard at them all, but wanted none to suffer at the expense of the other.'

Her words flushed her cheeks again and she looked out of the kitchen window into the distance beyond the bushes – beyond the trees, beyond the houses, way, way further on, to a place called nowhere. Her eyes filled up with tears as she cried for her man.

Kennedy put his arm around her, pulled her towards him and rocked her gently back and forth – gently encouraging her to let out her hurt.

Chapter Thirteen

Kennedy hung around the Berry household for a short time after concluding his interview with Sheila Berry. He had some more questions to ask but they weren't urgent and would be better left for another time. He left them going about the job of picking up the pieces of their lives.

WPC Coles remained behind. It had not actually been defined anywhere just exactly what the police force were meant to do in such instances, but Kennedy felt that having the WPC stay there and being available left a subtle message with Sheila that she had a connection with the outside world, that, in some way, she was not entirely alone.

Walking back over Primrose Hill to the office, Kennedy thought that this was definitely the best time of the year to be on the hill – not a sunbather in sight and only the rarest of dog-walkers. The air was tight and sharp on the nostrils. He pulled his collar up around his ears, thinking that the Crombie is a great coat. Kennedy didn't mind being out in the cold but he did like to be protected against it with warm clothes. He was wearing the Crombie for the first time, although he had bought it over a year ago; Kennedy did that a lot. He hated to wear new clothes, so he would buy the clothes he liked and keep them for about six months to a year before wearing them, thus avoiding their newness. Kennedy liked to be comfortable but not noticeable in his clothes. He had always been like that – even as a kid he could remember having his father put brown polish on the white soles of his new sandals to ensure they would not look new, only to have his friends say on first appearance, 'Ah, look – Kennedy's got new sandals.'

The time taken for his walk was spent running all the information around in his head. It was like having only a few pieces of a jigsaw puzzle available to you when you obviously need a full set before you can get any sense of what the picture is about. But Kennedy felt the more he studied the pieces he had, the better chance he had of seeing if, in fact, there actually was a picture to see.

He exited the hill on the corner of Albert Terrace and Prince Albert Road. Crossing Prince Albert Road at the junction of Princess Street took him to the bridge leading to Cumberland Basin. Kennedy leaned on the railings of the bridge and surveyed the scene once more.

There was no sign of the Sailing Diamond or of its two-man crew, so after a few minutes' meditation – and absolutely no flash of inspiration – he began the quarter-mile walk back to North Bridge House. It was time to brief his superior officer and make some decisions.

Superintendent Thomas Castle was happy to have men like Kennedy on his team. In fact, he would be even happier to have more officers like Kennedy around. He liked detectives who aspired to be just that, detectives. It helped make the superintendent look good and enabled him to get on with his primary purpose: further promotion.

Castle's office was not as snug as Kennedy's, at least not to Kennedy's eyes. The superintendent spent all his time trying to move into bigger and better offices so he never had the opportunity to make his current one homely, livable or comfortable.

'Kennedy – come in, sit down. What's the news on this Berry case?'

Kennedy sat down in front of the superintendent's desk, recognising from the tone of the greeting that this will be a 'straight in, quick discussion of facts, and straight back out again' kind of meeting. He had hoped for a cup of tea but when no offer of one was made he decided it would be better to get on with the business in hand.

He produced a notebook from his inside pocket. The pages were crisp and the writing neat and easy to read. Kennedy's notebook is not your standard-issue police notebook. It's slightly larger and opens from right to left, not top to bottom. It's encased in a thin, brown leather-wallet affair – thin enough not to bulk his pocket awkwardly. Kennedy may use two, or sometimes even three, refills per case. His writings are more notes to himself – a record of his thoughts and what he feels to be important quotes from some of the witness statements. He updates his notebook two or three times a day. He does this in private as he feels self-conscious writing in public.

'Well, sir,' he began, 'Dr Edmund Berry: healthy, happy, very happy, semi-prosperous and far-sighted. But on this occasion it appears that he acts completely out of character and consumes a great deal of alcohol and ends up at the bottom of Regent's Canal at the Cumberland Basin. A witness may or may not have heard him jump, fall or be pushed in.'

'Yes, yes,' interrupted the superintendent, 'Accident, murder or suicide?'

'Well, sir – I'm suspicious to say the least. I can't feel comfortable with suicide. Firstly, there was no note found. Not every suicide leaves a note but Dr Berry cared for his family, his wife and his son. So if he did wish to end his own life then I'm sure he would have made arrangements, note and will. I've checked and he hasn't made a will. Secondly, he apparently didn't usually drink very much. On the rare occasion he did, it was always red wine. Yet, a large quantity of spirits were found in his body. He got his sugar-fix from chocolate as he had a very sweet tooth, one of those chocolate-coated peanut freaks apparently. A box of the same was found in his pocket, and it was confirmed by his wife.

'Thirdly, he would not have walked to Cumberland Basin. He certainly didn't drive there. No car keys were found in his pockets and DS Irvine tells me that his car is in its usual place in the hospital car-park. Either he took the bus – unlikely – or else someone must have driven him there or else taken him there by force. Fourthly, being a doctor, he could easily have found an easier way of taking his life. Jumping into a cold, dark and dirty canal at seven o'clock in the morning can't top the list of how to take one's life. Fifthly, if he did want to drown himself, I doubt if he'd have done it there: the water's only four feet deep where he was found; he could have stood up in it.'

'But surely he wouldn't have known that until he jumped in, and your witness did hear a splash,' interrupted the superintendent.

'True and true – but we don't know if the splash was actually him hitting the water though, sir.'

'Heyee.' The Super drew the air back through his teeth. 'Do you have any hunches, Kennedy?'

Kennedy paused for a few seconds, trying to form his words.

'It's just that he seemed to be part of a very stable family life, I think. That's all I know. I have a feeling that he did not or would not commit suicide. His wife… his son… I don't think he would have left them this way.'

Superintendent Castle could see that Kennedy was troubled over this. He needed the meeting to end; he was late for his next and more important appointment. So, though he wasn't sure this was anything more than a suicide, he gave Kennedy his blessing to carry on.

'Okay. Spend some time on this and see what you can come up with. Keep me posted. The inquest is set for Friday so let's have an update before then, my son.'

The Superintendent stood up and put on the jacket that hung on the back of his chair. The meeting had ended.

Chapter Fourteen

'**D**r Burgess will see you now,' the young nurse announced. She wore a blue and white uniform, starched to crispness, and had pinned upon her chest the nurses medal – the upside-down fob watch.

'A terrible thing this, Inspector.' Dr Spencer Burgess greeted Kennedy by shaking his hand, before closing the door behind him and guiding him to the visitor's chair, all in one fine, orchestrated movement.

From the exterior, the hospital looked as grand and elegant as the St Pancras British Rail mainline station. A magnificent building, putting to shame a lot of the newer ones in its shadow. But inside All Saints Hospital, everything was antiseptic clean, if a tad tatty. Trying to fit too many people into too small a space created a shoe-box effect.

Dr Burgess obviously had some influence and importance in the hospital power-structure. He had what appeared to add up to a total of three shoe-boxes – one for his receptionist/secretary and the remaining two converted into one space to act as his office and consulting room.

The walls were covered with diplomas, certificates and pictures. Burgess had two large bookcases along the partition wall and they were packed to bursting with journals, textbooks and papers. At a quick glance, Kennedy noticed that more than a few of the books referred to eyes – obviously, his field of work.

His desk, a grand affair, was placed close to one of the large windows. Unfortunately, this majestic arched window could only be fully appreciated from outside the building. Internally, what once had been one very large floor had now been made into three – the result being that the window in Dr Burgess' room stretched from floor to ceiling, where one could see the beginning of the arch.

Burgess stiffly took his seat. A small man, he was immaculately 'turned out', as Kennedy's mother would say. His hair was short with a knife-edge parting – not a single hair out of place. He had a clean, well-shaven face except for some unfortunate bum-fluff on his top lip. He looked liked a two-shirt-a-day man – this must have been his blue-shirt period. His tie was of the old-school variety.

His desk echoed his personal fastidiousness. Pencils – well-sharpened – were lined up in a neat row, parallel to the righthand side of his desk. In the middle of the desk, directly in front of the doctor, was a pile of papers demanding his immediate attention. To the left of the desk was a photograph of the doctor and a good-looking, mature model-type woman – presumably his wife. The photo showed Burgess in casual attire, or as casual as he could go. The photograph seemed to be positioned so that his guests could admire it as much as the doctor clearly did himself.

He opened a drawer to his left and took out a clean crystal-glass ashtray containing a pack of Benson and Hedges, and offered one to Kennedy who, as a non-smoker, refused. The doctor lit-up. With the cigarette placed between his first and second fingers and using the thumb and first finger of the same hand, he removed a piece of tobacco that had lodged between his teeth.

His impeccably manicured fingers moved the papers on his desk slightly to the left and then back to their original position. He was ready to begin.

'How can I help you, Inspector?' His voice appeared unused to speaking insignificant things. It had a commanding tone, probably cultivated, but used so often it appeared perfectly natural.

Kennedy decided that he was in charge of the interview. He decided that he would conduct it – so, he allowed the silence to hang between them. He raised his hand to his mouth, as if in thought, but to ensure that Burgess did not break the silence.

Kennedy began. 'Your wife, Doctor?' His eyes were fixed on the photograph.

'What? Oh, yes… yes.'

'Been married long?' Kennedy asked quietly.

'Pardon?'

'Been married long?' repeated Kennedy.

'Twelve years – yes, twelve years last September,' replied the Doctor, becoming slightly fidgety.

Kennedy now took a left turn on Burgess. 'How long have you known Dr Berry?'

'Oh, now let me see. He came here as an SHO…'

'An SHO, Doctor?' interrupted Kennedy.

'Sorry – a Senior House Officer,' explained Burgess, labouring the words ever so slightly before continuing – 'And he passed his exams to become a registrar so that would make it about… let's see… just under four years.'

'Did you know him well? Did you mix much socially?'

'I knew him well professionally, Inspector, but we rarely met socially. We have – had – a different circle of friends.'

'Had he any troubles you were aware of, Doctor?'

'None that affected his work… except…'

'Yes, Doctor?' prompted Kennedy.

'Well, I'm not going to tell you anything you won't hear from other people; you may well have already heard about it.'

Burgess appeared to hesitate.

'Go on, Doctor?' Kennedy said, a notch or two up in volume.

'Well, Inspector – a short time ago Dr Berry was... well, he had a patient die on him in rather unexplained circumstances. The hospital is still carrying out an investigation, so none of us at this point in time really know what happened.'

'You're referring to the Susanne Collins death are you?'

'Oh, you're already aware of it. Well, I suppose that is your job. Yes, a terrible case. It's dreadful when something like that happens. Sometimes you have to fight to win a patient and often the chances are at best even – but when you lose a case which seemed pretty straightforward, it must be effecting. I do not think that anyone held Dr Berry responsible , and I am sure he acted in a proper and competent manner.'

'Did Dr Berry drink a lot?'

Burgess looked puzzled.

'As in alcohol, Doctor?' Kennedy clarified.

'Well, I do believe he liked his wine – bit of a wine buff on the old French reds, I hear. But you should check with someone who knew him better.'

'When did you last see Dr Berry?'

'The late shift the night before last. He was due to relieve me the morning he died. He just didn't show up. It wasn't until much later in the day that we learnt what had happened. I was told the news when I awoke yesterday afternoon. You know, Inspector – we deal a lot with death in our work here, but when it happens to someone you know, someone you work with, it hits you in a different way. It's kind of a permanent distraction – if you know what I mean?'

'Yes, I think I do,' replied Kennedy, thinking that it was a different kind of distraction altogether for Sheila Berry.

They both thought their thoughts for a few moments.

It was Kennedy who interrupted their silence: 'Well, Dr Burgess – I'll let you get on with your job and I with mine.'

Burgess rose stiffly from his chair. Kennedy thought he noticed a flash of pain in his eyes. 'You all right, Doctor?'

'It's just my back, Inspector – I've put it out again. I'll have the osteopath do some work on it for me later – loosen it up a bit.'

They walked towards the door. Kennedy opened it but as he was about to leave the room he turned back to face Burgess. 'Doctor – do you think that Dr Berry was the type of person who would commit suicide by jumping into a dirty, cold canal?'

'Inspector – we never really know what the people around us are capable of. We only know what the people around us want us to think that they are capable of. In short, nothing would surprise me, nothing at all.'

'Sorry, Doctor – that's not what I meant. What I meant was if someone like the doctor – or any doctor for that matter – wanted to take their life, wouldn't there be a million easier ways to do it with medicine?'

'Yes, I suppose so – but then again, someone in such a state probably would not think as logically as you do, Inspector.'

They parted, the picture none the clearer for either of them.

Chapter Fifteen

'**K**ennedy, your problem is that you dream too much. Hello in there,' ann rea said, waving her hand in front of his eyes. 'Is anyone there? Can you come back to the real world please?'

'Oh, sorry. Sorry, ann rea,' murmured Kennedy snapping out of his thoughts. 'I was miles away, I really was.'

They were sitting in The Queens, later that same day.

'What's on your mind, Christy?' ann rea said with genuine tenderness. She usually addressed him as Kennedy but now, she used his christian name.

'I just can't get a fix on this Berry thing at all. I feel foul play was involved. But that's the problem, I've nothing more to go on than a feeling. I have several hunches but not one scrap of proof to suggest anything other than the fact that he had a few drinks too many, was out walking along the canal in the early hours of the morning, stumbled, and ended up in the water. You know, it doesn't even have to be a suicide or a murder, it could be something as simple as an accident. It could, ann rea – it could,' he said, trying to convince himself as much as her.

She smiled. 'Ah, but you don't think so, do you?' Before he could answer, she added, 'It's getting too busy in here. Let's go for a walk. Fancy that Kennedy?'

His mood brightened. He enjoyed being in her company. It felt natural, comfortable – maybe too comfortable. At times, that was his biggest fear, that she would end up treating him as a mate, as a brother-type figure. And that would be it, they would be doomed to being 'just good friends'. Kennedy often wondered at that – how could good friends be *just* good friends? A bit of a contradiction in terms, he thought.

Once that 'mates' kind of a relationship started, it would be hard if not impossible, to move it over into the romantic area – and that was exactly the direction Kennedy wanted his relationship with ann rea to develop. But the sad thing was that he just did not have a clue what he should be doing to achieve this. At least their relationship was fun, so Kennedy's only plan was to hang around and see where they ended up.

They joined the buzz on the street. It was one of those nights when the streets around Primrose Hill come alive: not with hundreds of people but with just enough to provide an atmosphere of people with purpose.

An old man, maybe with a military background, is walking his dog, his left hand attempting to cope with the leash and with a news-paper-cone full of chips. His other hand is used to select his chips singularly, and the hot air in his mouth creates puffs of steam each time his mouth accepts a new one. He talks to his dog between bites.

Three young teenagers – two of them male, each trying to impress the lone female – display their Kids-On-The-Block, New York-style dress-sense (or lack of it) and are attempting the famous 'walk with attitude'. This doesn't quite come off for one for the males, who keeps tripping over his trousers. But better tripping on his trousers than tripping, full-stop, thinks Kennedy.

Two old dears, out for what might be their nightly walk along their regular route. They dress Norma Batty-style – humble but clean – and have obviously been together for so long, they no longer need to talk to each other. They may even be sisters.

There are several double-parked cars, the owners in buying fish and chips from the family-run fish and chip shop. If the car owners are not after fish and chips then they're probably picking up some booze from one of the two off-licences. The one on the same side of the road as the fish and chip shop does excellent fresh pasta, as Kennedy advises ann rea.

Even the launderette seems to have a vibe going. It is full of customers who are not really dressed properly for public appearance but who possibly feel that going to the launderette is not really going out in public. The inhabitants of this establishment usually keep to their own space, getting on with the job in hand, perhaps thinking, If I don't look at other people's clothes they won't look at mine, and mine are a bit dirty. At the moment ann rea and Kennedy pass, they are sharing a joke that neither of the two walkers would want to be party to.

Odette's is packed, warm and expensive. Two people, a couple in their early thirties, are leaving, their faces aglow from wine and good food. It crosses Kennedy's mind that later, in the privacy of one of their homes, their bodies will be aglow with passion. He envies them.

ann rea points to some graffiti at the bottom of two posters on the window of what used to be the Fiat showroom. There are two posters, side by side, both with photographs – not David Bailey shots, mind you. The first bears the legend *Vote Labour*, the other demands a vote for the Tories. Underneath some wag had written, 'Vote for neither – you'll only encourage them.'

To the right of Odette's is Primrose Hill Books, the London book-store with the largest number of local authors, and next to that, the

Polish café which seems to specialise in customers with thick skin. At this minute, it's closed and two of the sombre staff are cleaning up.

Across the street, Kennedy spots the local rare-books dealer and songwriter, Niatat Armikit. Legend has it that she lives somewhere around Primrose Hill. Kennedy tries hard not to stare because he knows it's rude and must be happening to her all the time, but it is hard not to stare – she's so naturally beautiful. ann rea tells Kennedy that she's interviewed Niatat on quite a few occasions and has always found her polite, intelligent and funny: quite unusual for music business interviewees.

ann rea linked her arm through Kennedy's and guided him off towards the hill. 'Come on, Kennedy – let's see what we can see from the top of Primrose Hill.'

'Good idea,' answered Kennedy, realising where he had been mentally and snapping out of it. That's the problem with spending too much time with oneself, he was thinking – you become too used to being sad or even finding a solace with sadness. To the outside world, you may look dark or depressed but inside you're dealing with it. He turned to ann rea: 'I'm poor company, I know.'

'I wouldn't say so, Kennedy. You're just more used to being on your own.'

'Ha , now there's a thing,' he chuckled.

'What, the truth?'

'No. Those two over there.' He nodded over to their right at a couple leaning against a tree, who were inside each other's overcoats and drinking from each other's mouths.

ann read dug Kennedy in the ribs and pulled him up the hill.

If outside The Queens they had seen a 'street' buzz, then up here they saw a 'city' buzz. A clear night on the top of Primrose Hill gives you a sense of the London which is missing from both street level and daytime.

'I've been checking into the Collins story – both Norman Collins – Susanne Collins' brother – and William Jackson – her boyfriend – have been doing quite a bit of stirring on this. Supposedly, they're threatening to sue the hospital for millions and apparently they were originally trying to bring criminal charges against Dr Berry.'

'Have you spoken to either of them yet, Kennedy?' enquired ann rea.

'No , not yet. Norman Collins lives in Derby and William Jackson is on compassionate leave from school and is 'out of town' or lost. No-one seems to know where he is. DS Irvine is trying to track him down now.' He thought for a moment and then continued. 'You think there might be something in it?'

'Oh, I don't know, Kennedy. That's your job – but surely the unexplained death of a loved one must provide some kind of motive?'

'Could be, could be. There's still too many missing links in this thing but tomorrow we should be able to make some ground. It's just that for a couple of days now, we've dug deep and come up with absolutely zero. Castle will be wanting some facts soon and if I can't give him anything, he'll want me to return to the backlog. Are you doing a piece on this case, ann rea?'

'I probably will at some point, but don't worry, Kennedy – I won't land you in trouble.'

'No, no. I didn't mean that.'

'I know you didn't. Anyway, I'd run anything I was going to do past you first. I'm not looking for stories, Kennedy. I can't compete with the *Evening Standard*, LBC and GLR. They can all beat me for a story by hours and sometimes even by a week. I have to try and find a different view – the full story, the complete picture. I always find a well-composed picture far more interesting, pleasing and lasting than a five-day wonder. Know what I mean?'

They sat down on one of the benches on the top of Primrose Hill and enjoyed the view. People came by, sometimes in threes and fours, but mostly couples, and tried to pick out the various London landmarks. They would stay for five or ten minutes and then move on.

'Ah, shit! Kennedy!' she shouted, sliding over the bench closer to him.

They were touching.

'What's the matter?'

'That bleedin' great dog,' she said, indicating an Irish Wolfhound. 'I can't stand them.'

The dog was obviously taking its owner out for a walk and had probably left the poor woman or poor man panting halfway up the hill. The large (as in extraordinarily large) dog was approaching Kennedy and ann rea. The closer the dog came, the closer ann rea squeezed towards Kennedy. He put his arm around her and used the other hand to pat the dog which proved to be a big softy. Big Softy grew bored and ran off to do some gardening, which in his case meant digging, planting and watering. Kennedy felt ann rea relax against him. He didn't move his arm.

They looked at each other, neither sure what to do. Their heads started to move ever so slightly closer to each other – just like in the movies. He calculated that, at their current speed, in approximately fifteen seconds their lips would meet. He tried to remember when he had last cleaned his teeth. He was just about to close his eyes for the final few inches when, all of a sudden, ann rea broke free, jumped up and said, 'Come on Kennedy – I better get you home. I don't want the Camden CID on my case!'

Chapter Sixteen

R ecorded highlights of the previous scene ran through Kennedy's mind's eye, early the following morning. He was in his office, cup of tea in hand, re-living the moments of his near-glory and staring at his 'Cumberland Basin' case noticeboard.

The noticeboard was littered with sheets of paper, some bearing the names of the main players in the case – Edmund Berry, Martin Shaw and Peter Blackburn (the name by which Junior was known to the taxman and his bank manager). Susanne Collins was up there, too – as were her brother, Norman and boyfriend, William Jackson. There were photos of Dr Berry and Susanne Collins, courtesy of Mrs Berry and the *Camden News Journal* respectively. The board also displayed two photographs taken at the spot where Berry was fished out. Kennedy had lines drawn to delineate the connections between the people listed on his board, such as they were. He'd also listed the key details concerning Berry's drowning:

7–8am, V. drunk, Body marked, Patient dead.

With the help of Staff Nurse Rose Butler and Sheila Berry, he had pieced together a timetable detailing Berry's last known movements and that was up on the board, too.

Kennedy saw Mrs Berry on most days and he was inspired by her courage and her ability to deal with the situation. Staff Nurse Butler he liked – she made him tea, and they chatted quite a bit – Kennedy felt that the more he grew to know her, the looser her tongue would become.

On the day before his death, Berry awoke around two in the afternoon, having been on duty until 2am the previous night. He spent what Americans call 'quality time' with his family, dining with them until about four in the afternoon.

Berry said goodbye to his wife and son at 5.45pm and drove the short distance to the hospital. This journey usually took him anything up to ten minutes. Berry was on call as opposed to being on duty – that is, he was back-up or standing by in case of an emergency. This meant that he could occupy himself as he so desired until such time as his services were required by one of the JHOs. This usually happened when the outpatients unit was dealing with more than one emergency at once and the duty-SHO was occupied with another case.

Staff Nurse Butler saw Berry throughout the early part of the evening. He was talking to people and then catching up on some paperwork in the staff common-room until nine o'clock, when she joined him there to watch the BBC news. They chatted for a few minutes after the news while they finished their respective coffee and tea. At that point, he retired to his cot in the rest-room and she went about her duties.

The on-call doctor was allowed to sleep. In fact, they were encouraged to do so. Berry could be alert quicker by catnapping and that is what he usually did.

Staff Nurse Butler never saw Berry again. He was due to finish his on-call obligations at 2am. The usual routine was for the doctors either to set an alarm that woke them at the end of their shift – at which point they would go home – or sleep on through to the morning. Berry usually chose the latter, deciding not to ruin his wife's sleep as well. So, he would catnap on his back until the end of his shift and then turn over for deeper sleep on his side. Sleep was precious to doctors – more so now that they were being called on for more and longer shifts – so the wisest of them took every opportunity to make up their sleep deficit to guarantee some kind of sharpness while on duty.

Dr Berry died in the canal at Cumberland Basin between seven and eight o'clock that morning. What had happened to him between 2am and 7am? That was, of course, assuming that the doctor stayed in the hospital until the completion of his shift at 2am.

Kennedy studied Berry's timetable.

Monday 1st February

14.00	Wakes up at home
16.00	Dines with family
16.40	Departs for hospital
18.00	On-call shift begins
	Seen around hospital until
21.00	Watches TV news with SN Butler
21.40	Retires to cot in rest-room
	Naps until

Tuesday 2nd February

02.00	??? until
07.30	(ish) Drowns
10.00	Body recovered by Shaw and Junior

Berry had been in the cold, dirty water from seven o'clock until he was found at 10am by the crew of the Sailing Diamond, Martin Shaw and Junior.

'What happened to you, Doctor – between 2am and 7am?' Kennedy asked the photograph on his noticeboard, before he was disturbed by a gentle tapping on his door.

'Come in.'

'Good morning, guv.'

It was DS Irvine come a-calling. Kennedy greeted the lively Scot. 'Good morning, Jimmy. Come on in. How about a cup of tea?'

'Yes please, sir. Your tea does as much for me at this time of the day as a Glenfiddich does for me at the end.'

'Yes, Jimmy – I've noticed. Perhaps you should take your eyes down to a blood bank this morning and have them drained.'

They both laughed, a little, not a lot.

Kennedy's laugh dissolved into a smile as he continued with the enjoyable ritual of tea-making. After a few minutes, he turned to his assistant. 'I suppose we should talk to Collins and Jackson today. I also want to visit the hospital again and talk some more with Staff Nurse Butler. I'd also like someone to chat with Martin Shaw and Junior, again – just in case we missed something or they missed telling us something. Send DC Milligan – he's got initiative. Tell him to talk them through the sequence, again. It's surprising what's left lurking in the back of the brain and will stay there until someone prods it out.'

Irvine was infected by Kennedy's energy. 'Have you got anything, sir? Are you on to something?'

Kennedy replied quietly: 'I just feel there's something out there waiting for us – just one thing. Just one thing, Jimmy. I'll take it either way – proof of foul play or proof of suicide. It's there, so let's find it.'

Kennedy handed Irvine a cup of tea. 'Here,' he said. 'Take this to fortify your resolve.'

Chapter Seventeen

WPC Coles drove Kennedy the short distance over to St Pancras All Saints Hospital. She thought it unusual that a name should have two saints in its title. She was enjoying her time on this case and was hoping that if she impressed enough it could be the start of some CID work. Not that she minded the day-to-day uniform police work, but she had joined up with an ambition of moving through the ranks to Chief Inspector and further.

Coles had a passion for this work but she was aware of how hard it was for a woman to have a successful career in the police force, a disgraceful thing to have to admit to in the latter years of the twentieth century. She did, however, hope that the discrimination, with its unfair work-load, would make her a better detective.

'So, when we reach the hospital, WPC Coles,' began Kennedy, breaking into her thought process, 'I'm going to chat some more to Staff Nurse Butler and I want you to check around with the other nurses and see what you can pick up.'

'Is there anything in particular you need to know, sir?' Coles replied, as she changed down gears to stop at a red traffic light, a few streets away from the hospital.

'No, nothing specific. Just see what you can pick up. I'm looking for anything, any leads on this, and I'm assuming that if there's anything to know about the goings-on in this hospital then the nurses will know it. Find out what you can about Doctors Berry and Burgess. Get the gossip on Susanne Collins – any rumours, any theories, any scraps at all – that's how desperate I am. I'll settle for any scraps you can pick up. There has to be something out there that we're not getting. All the routine work has come up with nothing so far.'

She had not noticed that the lights had changed. The car immediately behind was aware of the WPC in front and sat quietly but some dickhead – white shirt, red braces, in a Porsche behind the quiet driver – started hooting his horn and effing and blinding and waving his arms out of his window to create rude signs.

'Give me a couple of seconds and then pull in over there beside that telephone box,' Kennedy said, as he exited the car and paced back two cars to the offending driver.

Kennedy flashed his ID card and requested that the driver pull in behind the WPC.

'Now then, sir,' Kennedy began, 'what seems to be the trouble?'

The driver was typically indignant – more front than Sainsbury's. Greased-back hair, big blue-framed glasses and music blaring loud. The music's not loud because our friend Richard Head likes it, but because to play it loud is a statement – a way of getting attention. He was definitely receiving some attention now. 'The lights had changed and your car hadn't moved, mate.'

'That, sir, is not an offence. Noise pollution, on the other hand, is.' These people really rattled Kennedy's cage, but although he would like to take out the frustrations of the Berry case on this product of the nineties, he could not and he would not. But he could waste some of this irritable man's precious time. 'Present your insurance and driving licence at the front desk at Camden police station – at the top of Parkway – within the next twenty-four hours.'

'I can't man – I'm going to the coast!'

'And which coast would that be, sir? Brighton or Bristol?' Kennedy responded. 'If I were you, sir, I would delay my trip to the coast until you drop your insurance off in Camden. I'll radio in your details now and unless they hear from you within twenty-four hours, we'll issue a warrant for your arrest. I'm sure you'll find that much more inconvenient.'

Kennedy felt some satisfaction for a little while – then he felt bad about having played such games, deserved or not. When he returned to the car, he asked WPC Coles the difference between a pigeon and a yuppie.

'I don't know, sir. What is the difference?' she replied, somewhat surprised.

'A pigeon can still leave a deposit on a Porsche.'

Kennedy laughed as loud as Coles.

Shortly afterwards, they were walking into the hospital in pursuit of more information concerning the Cumberland Basin case. Kennedy told Coles that he didn't believe Berry had taken his own life.

Their timing was perfect. As they arrived Staff Nurse Rose Butler was about to commence her tea-break and she happily agreed to share it with Kennedy. Rose Butler was gregarious, she found it easy to talk to new people and she had taken a shine to Kennedy.

'You better watch yourself or there'll be talk around here, you'll do my reputation the world of good,' she chuckled as they settled down at a quiet table in the staff canteen, Rose with her tea, round of egg and cress sandwiches and an apple. Kennedy settled for tea – slightly too strong, known as stewed tea – and two Jacob's chocolate-coated orange-flavoured biscuits.

'So, is there much of that goes on here?' he began.

'Oh, you are awful.' she Emeryised.

'But I like you,' he joined in. 'But seriously,' he continued, 'gossip is what I'm after; any hospital gossip?'

'Same as everywhere else, I suppose, Christy. Now, you don't mind me calling you Christy, do you?

He smiled his assent, not sure he had a choice in the matter.

'Good. It' s much nicer than Detective Inspector or Mr Kennedy. Now then – gossip. Yes, of course we have tittle-tattle around here.' Her eyes broke into a devilish smile. Her jet-black hair was pulled back and tied up in some unique form that joined into and under her nurse's cap – lots of hair clips and lots of hard work getting all that together for sure, thought Kennedy.

'Was Dr Berry badly shaken by the Susanne Collins death?'

Rose finished chewing her first mouthful of egg and cress sandwich, and took a swig of tea to wash it down before answering. 'Totally – totally shook up. Devastated, more like, I'd say. It was completely unexpected. I wasn't on duty when she was admitted but I saw her the following morning when I was doing the rounds of the wards with the duty-doctor.'

'And she looked fine?' Kennedy inquired.

'Yes, she looked fine – chirpy enough.'

'Do they know exactly what happened yet?'

'No. It's quite fascinating really. They've been carrying out an investigation ever since it happened. They took all the notes and all the records and files – but nothing. Not even a mutter.'

'Does anybody have any idea what happened?' Kennedy inquired.

'No, not really. It's too much of a madhouse in here. You work on so many cases and because of the duty rosters you rarely see a case the whole way through. If patients are in here for a week or more, you start to become more familiar with them. But if they're only in here for three or four days they'll rarely see the same nurse twice. That's why we place such importance on the files – to ensure that the treatment can continue successfully, we hope. But no is the short answer. No-one has any idea what happened to the Collins girl.'

'Can the hospital be sued for damages?'

'Yes, if negligence can be proved. And I hear two of the relatives are kicking up quite a storm. The brother and the boyfriend, I believe.' Rose quietened her voice in a conspiratorial manner. 'The brother had a meeting with the hospital General Manager, Alexander Bowles, and apparently there was a lot of screaming and shouting and the brother roughed up the office a bit. Mr Bowles was very shaken after the brother left. He nearly slammed the door off its hinges as he was leaving. Screaming about a cover-up and how you're not going to get away with it, you've not heard the last of me, that sort of thing. A few of the nurses who saw him leave were very scared: apparently his eyes were all but bursting out of their sockets. But I feel sorry for him. He's lost a loved one and now he's alone… all that anger… poor man.'

'Is the hospital insured against these sort of lawsuits?' Kennedy inquired.

'I imagine so – but Mr Bowles could tell you better than I.'

'And Dr Burgess – what can you tell me about him?'

'Hmm – ambitious, very ambitious. None of the nurses like him. He treats us as inferiors, frequently shouting at us and blaming us for his own mistakes.'

'Does he make many mistakes?'

'We all do, Christy. With the hours we have to work and the amount we have to do, it's impossible not to make some mistakes. It's just a case of trying to keep your wits about you to some degree, ignoring the pressure, checking other people's work, having people check yours.'

'What about Dr Berry? Did he make any major blunders?' inquired Kennedy.

'No, not that I'm aware of. He was a great doctor, on his way to becoming a brilliant one. Cared a lot about his work. He always seemed to be trying to keep in good shape. Took lots of naps, unlike some of them. The things they get up to when they are meant to be on call, some of them even nip down to the local and you have to bleep them there if anything comes up. Some of the doctors have more… ah, shall we say, energetic ways of spending their on-call times.' Rose smiled another of those devilish smiles.

She thought for some time before continuing. 'But going back to Dr Berry, that's why this Collins case is even more surprising. I can't see Dr Berry breaking procedure and making a mistake – not a bad mistake, certainly. Bad enough for someone to die. That's what's been troubling me. There must have been some mystery illness, something else present that caused her to die.'

'But surely that would have shown up in the autopsy?'

'Yes, it should have, but, as I say, we've had no news from Mr Bowles. Perhaps he'll tell you, Christy.'

'Maybe he will. I'm seeing him later. Let's go back to Dr Berry. Did he ever fool around with any of the nurses?'

'No, no – definitely not. That's not something you could keep quiet around here. The bush telegraph beats in here and it beats very loud. No doubt he wouldn't have had a problem if he'd tried; he was very handsome, lots of charm. A great man. But then again, you see, Christy, the great men don't fool around because they're all either married or gay, aren't they?'

Kennedy chuckled. 'What about Dr Burgess – any dirt swept under his carpet?'

'No, he's too ambitious, too hungry to get on to even notice women. They say he's due for promotion shortly and this is the big step for him. He becomes the big fish. Next, I suppose, he'll be looking for a bigger pond.'

Rose paused before going on.

'With Dr Burgess, the gossip's all about the other side of the family!' she said teasingly.

'What do you mean, Rose?'

'The wife, Amelia Burgess...' She hesitated, perhaps baiting Kennedy.

'Yes – and?'

'Well, she's a stunner – very beautiful and no-one has ever been able to work out what she saw in Dr Burgess to swear "till death us do part".'

Kennedy was puzzled and bemused.

'Come on, Christy – he's no Robert Redford. He's not even James Irvine for that matter,' she smiled, a hint of naughtiness creeping through, 'and the doctor doesn't even seem interested in his wife. Another possession or career move, if you ask me, Christy. Apparently, she's been playing away from home. Very discreet, as you would expect from someone of her class, and no-one knows who it is.'

'Is Dr Burgess aware of Amelia's... erm... wanderings?'

'I don't know. Mind you, with him, I wouldn't be surprised if he was turning a blind eye to it, it might suit him and help make up for his own lack of interest, if you know what I mean.' She winked and tipped her nose with her forefinger. 'As long as she's there to be on his arm when needed. Apparently, it's been going on for quite some time now.'

'Various men or just the one?'

'Well again, Christy, no-one really knows but it's felt that it's the one man and quite serious. This is, of course, all based on putting two and two together and getting the result you want.'

'Hmm, interesting. I'm not sure it means anything in my case but it certainly is interesting,' Kennedy conjectured.

'Now, Christy, I've been ever so good with your questions so how's about you returning the favour and telling me all about Sergeant Irvine. Is he spoken for?'

'Not that I'm aware of,' Kennedy answered, more than slightly amused. 'Want me to put in a word or something?' he laughed.

'No, I'm quite capable of asking a man out if I'm interested in him. I just hate to waste time on married men or men that are "playing the field". I just wanted to make sure the coast was clear – he's delicious.'

She read the response on Kennedy's face.

'Ha, you think I'm wicked, now don't you? But there are so few good men around, you can't afford to hang about when one comes into the picture. It's a jungle out there, Christy, particularly being a nurse. You know what nurses are meant to be?'

'No, what's that, Rose?'

'Now come on, Christy, you're pulling my leg, or maybe you're innocent enough to be telling the truth. Well, when you tell men – some men – you're a nurse, normal, reasonable men turn into animals. Animals, there's no other word for it. They seem to think that nurses are all wanton, frustrated nymphomaniacs. You should see their faces light up when you tell them that you're a nurse. It's got to the point where at parties I no longer tell strange men what I do for a living.'

'So, what do you say you are, Rose, a nun?'

'Now be off with you, Christy, and stop wasting any more of my time.' Rose laughed as she stood up from the table and took her dirty dishes to the return hatch. 'See you around,' she smiled to Kennedy across the canteen.

Chapter Eighteen

The following morning, Kennedy was attending the inquest into the death of Dr Edmund Berry. Twenty minutes had elapsed since he presented his evidence – his beliefs, his thoughts, his fears – and he awaited the verdict.

Various other people, including Drs Taylor and Burgess, had also given evidence.

Kennedy was feeling the hardness of the wooden seats. He shifted his weight from his right to his left side, trying to find some comfort.

ann rea was in the press box. Now that he was able to observe her from a distance, he felt he could fully appreciate her grace and beauty. That could be the problem of being up close to someone a lot, you tended to take their looks for granted. At this stage in his life, Kennedy was not sure how much liking someone had to do with how they looked.

The coroner was rattling on and on but Kennedy had noticed that since he started to focus his attention on ann rea, his seat had become considerably more comfortable. She dressed *sensibly*, that was the word. Everything she wore looked great – her clothes suited her but were not loud. Nor did her clothes try to flatter her femininity. She wore a little make-up very effectively.

Now, staring at her across the room, a lump rose in his throat. He felt increasingly attracted to her. Absurd though it may sound, he felt he could happily spend the rest of his life with her. That was a feeling he had only experienced once before in his life. He had been twenty-one and the relationship had turned out to be a total disaster. He had doubted that he would ever have that feeling again in his life, but here he was again, feeling the same about someone he had only just met and could not find a way to move off first-base with.

He continued to gawk at her and ann rea seemed to become somewhat uncomfortable, as though she were aware of his thoughts. She avoided his eyes and became preoccupied with her notebook, but she did not relax again.

The coroner's voice, increasing in volume, brought Kennedy back to his senses and his current priority. 'And so the events at Cumberland Basin on the morning of Tuesday 2nd February 1992 suggest to me that I must pronounce an open verdict and instruct Camden CID to continue their investigation into this matter.'

So, Kennedy had convinced the coroner that there was a reasonable doubt as to the means of Berry's death and he had sowed the seeds of doubt in Superintendent Castle's mind. Now all he had to do was go out and find his case and prove it.

The sad thing for Kennedy was that the inquest could just as easily have got it wrong and that the death could have been recorded as 'accidental' or 'death by his own hand' or 'death by misadventure'. That was Kennedy's main concern with the current judicial system. Whoever said that a coroner was always going to be correct? For that matter, who on earth ever said that a jury of twelve people were going to get it right each and every time?

That's why Kennedy liked his cases to be watertight; to be completely proven and finalised before they went to trial. Either a confession or a fully proven case, preferably both. He hated to depend on a clever lawyer winning – or losing.

The proceedings at an end, Sheila Berry came over to him, dressed all in black, keeping her composure behind dark glasses.

'Thank you, Inspector. I'm relieved that it wasn't recorded as a suicide – but I'll be even happier if you can find out exactly what happened.'

'Let's get out of here,' said Kennedy, leading her by the arm.

They made their way outside and turned left, heading towards Camden Town.

The silence was broken by Sheila Berry: 'I can't move on with my life until this part is concluded, completed. Does that make any sense to you?'

'Yes, it makes a lot of sense.'

For the first time he became aware of how stunning she looked – not beautiful, stunning. On the other occasions when Kennedy had seen her, she had been crying, and crying makes people look ugly. The more people cry the uglier they look.

They walked for another few minutes in silence. It was very cold, with a lush blue sky.

'I was wanting to ask you a few questions. Is that okay?' Kennedy began, as hesitant as a new-born foal.

'Yes. Yes, that's fine Inspector. What did you want to know?'

'Well, I was wondering if your husband ever talked to you about the Collins case.'

'We talked a bit about it, around the time it happened. He was pretty shaken up, you know. He couldn't believe it; he kept saying that she shouldn't have died. She just shouldn't have died. He went through it in his mind over and over again, trying to figure out what had happened. Then he stopped talking about it altogether. I thought it better to keep it out of his mind so I didn't ask him about it again.'

They had reached Camden Town.

'Do you want a coffee or tea or anything?' Kennedy asked.

Sheila Berry sensed that Kennedy wanted to talk some more so she agreed. They went into Café Delancey. She had a cappuccino, he a tea, and she remembered how much Kennedy liked tea.

'A good cup of tea here is it, Inspector?'

'It's okay, not the best. The Salt and Pepper does a better cup. The milk here is a bit too creamy. They probably have it for the coffee or else it's that horrible long-life milk. Mind you, they do a great rösti potato in here.'

'The cappuccino is superb – lots of cinnamon. I like that,' she said quietly.

He leant across the table. 'What I'm going to ask next may appear hurtful. I don't mean it to be but you must understand that I have to try and rule out certain avenues of enquiry, so that we can get on with what's relevant. Is that okay?'

'Yes, it's fine, it's okay. I really want to help. I'll do anything to find out what really happened to Eddie.' She braced herself for his question.

'Well… er… did he ever… did you ever think that Dr Berry was seeing another woman?' he eventually announced, his voice barely audible.

'No! Definitely not!' she blurted. After a pause, she continued, 'God, it must appear terribly naive to make such a rash statement. You see, Inspector, we were rather close, Eddie and I.' Now it was her turn to talk quietly. 'We enjoyed a gloriously intimate relationship and that's one of the things I miss the most.' She blushed.

'I don't mean to open up…'

'No, it's fine, Detective Inspector. It's good to talk about it. I don't mean to use you as a priest.'

They both smiled.

'But it seems natural – here, talking to you about it. That in a way seems kind of weird – talking to a policeman about my love-life with my husband. But I don't feel bad about it. I hope it doesn't make you feel uncomfortable?'

All Kennedy could do was grunt. Sheila Berry didn't know whether to take this as a 'yes' grunt or a 'no' grunt, so she continued: 'Anyway, we had an honest and exciting sexual relationship. I think I would have known when he was with me – you know, in that way – if he had been with someone else. We had both talked quite a bit when we first met about keeping each other happy, about not taking each other for granted. That probably sounds silly to you now.'

Kennedy indicated that it didn't.

'We were both looking forward to growing old together and enjoying ourselves a lot while doing so. I remember before I met Eddie, when I was between boyfriends, how I would be out and I would see these attractive couples together and I would think to myself, Why are these people out on the street? Don't they realise how lucky they are to have each other? They should be in the privacy of their homes, doing naughty things to each other. But then, when I did find a boyfriend and after the newness and the novelty wore off, I didn't think that anymore. You think enough is enough already, let's get out and walk around for a while. With Eddie, it was different: we never tired of each other. The last time we made love was as exciting as the first time. No, Inspector, we were close, enough to realise if either of us had been playing around.'

She downed the dregs of her cappuccino and began to look somewhat uncomfortable, so Kennedy paid the bill and they headed off towards Camden High Street.

'Sorry about that, I don't know what came over me. I suppose all this talking about Eddie and thinking about Eddie in that way unnerved me a bit. I'd like to go home now if you don't mind?'

'No, not at all, no problem. We'll pick up a cab down here by the corner.'

'You're... you're a good man,' she said quietly.

Kennedy took a few steps before answering, 'No,' he paused, 'but I am a good detective.'

Sheila Berry smiled and they continued their walk down into the bustle of the High Street.

'Look, there's a cab.'

Kennedy raised his arm to hail the passing taxi. He informed the driver of Sheila Berry's address and just as he was about to make his goodbyes, she said: 'One funny thing, it probably means nothing, but I found out from our solicitor, John Chappell, that Eddie had made an appointment to see him for the afternoon of the day he died. He didn't tell John what he wanted to see him about, just said that it was something he didn't want to discuss on the phone.'

She looked as if she were expecting Kennedy to know what this meant.

'Goodbye and thank you,' Kennedy said as she got in and he closed the door.

He walked back to North Bridge House, making a note of the name John Chappell in his notebook. Not a major lead by any means, but another person to talk to, another lead to follow, and one of these leads would eventually take him somewhere. Of that, he had no doubt.

Chapter Nineteen

Capital Gold was beaming out 'Dedicated Follower of Fashion' by The Kinks as Kennedy's internal buzzer went off, ruining the mood.

'Yes?' The slightest note of exasperation crept into his voice.

'Sir, it's DS Irvine here.'

'Yes?'

'We've located William Jackson, sir. He's apparently back at his flat. Do you want us to bring him in?'

'No, Jimmy. Let's you and I drive around there and have a chat with him at home, okay?'

'Okay, sir – I'll bring the car around to the front. See you there in five minutes?' Irvine couldn't work out why the DI seemed to be so impatient – perhaps there was someone with him in the room.

'All right, five minutes.'

The phone clicked dead, but too late – The Kinks' finest record had ended. Actually, Kennedy was not altogether sure if The Kinks' best record was 'Dedicated Follower of Fashion' or 'Waterloo Sunset'. But what did it matter? Both were great songs *and* great records, which was certainly not always the case. Shrugging and hauling himself to his feet, Kennedy unhooked his Crombie coat and his long, black scarf from behind the door and headed off to meet Irvine.

William Jackson lived in a tree-filled square, busy with children about their street games. It was a flat at the top of a white terraced house in Camden Square.

As Irvine rang the doorbell, he noticed Kennedy's fingers twitching.

'Hello, who's there?' an unsure voice answered.

'Mr Jackson?' Kennedy inquired.

'Yes.'

'This is Detective Inspector Christy Kennedy and Detective Sergeant James Irvine here. We're from Camden CID and we'd like to have a word with you.'

'Oh… oh, yes – I'll buzz you in. Come on in; all the way to the top flat,' said the distorting speaker fixed to the wall.

A few flights and a little oxygen-debt later, the two policemen came face to face with William Jackson outside his opened door. Both flashed their ID cards, as if following an unheard cue. William

Jackson looked at the cards but didn't really see them. Kennedy reflected that most people wouldn't know a police warrant card from a library card but they should make it their business to know.

Jackson looked younger than he probably was, the way Gary Lineker and Tom Cruise do. Jackson's chin hosted a seven-day stubble. He was dressed in black, baggy trousers and a grey, baggy, unmarked sweatshirt. He wore Chinese flip-flops instead of shoes. All his movements were tentative, in the way a young animal makes its first steps beyond the protection of its parents.

'Come in,' he announced, and as they did so he closed the door behind them.

The flat was a throwback to the crash-pads of the sixties – red-ballooned light-shades and dark walls. But instead of the Roundhouse, Moody Blues, Jimi Hendrix and Cream posters, the walls sported billsheets proclaiming The Clash, The Buzzcocks and The Undertones.

There were no proper seats, just bean-bags and cushions. A black-and-white TV with an indoor aerial supported the standard-issue record-player – no cassettes, no CD-player. Our friend Jackson was a vinyl-junkie – half of one wall, from floor to ceiling, was lined with records.

Judging by the hum from the speakers, he had obviously been playing a record when the two policemen had rung his doorbell. Jackson must have killed the noise by lifting the needle but Kennedy couldn't make out what the record was, as it spun around and around on the turntable.

'We're investigating the sudden death of Edmund Berry and we have a few questions to ask you,' said Kennedy, finding it impossible to find words that would have put Jackson at his ease before starting questioning.

William Jackson merely nodded.

'We believe you were the boyfriend of Susanne Collins?'

No answer, just a flicker of remembrance, a pain he wished he could forget.

'We...'

'You don't think I had anything to do with Berry's death, do you?' A little realisation setting in.

'We're just trying to find out what happened.'

'Who's trying to find out what happened to Susanne? Hey – tell me that, will you?' Jackson was becoming hyper, speaking like a boxer being interviewed at the conclusion of a successful fight. 'She never harmed anyone,' he continued. 'She didn't hurt anyone, she didn't deserve to die.'

He was now pacing the distance between himself and the detectives, muttering incoherently.

'We believe that the hospital is looking into the circumstances surrounding the death...' began Kennedy.

'Looking into it... looking into it!' interrupted Jackson. 'Come on, Mr Policeman – do you honestly expect me to believe that? Don't you see that it's a cover-up? It's a cover-up that's going on here. They're so busy protecting their own, the way they... the way you all do,'he spat.

Jackson was obviously used to having an audience. He had the pose of a crowd rabble-rouser, acting aggressively towards someone and having people back him up with chants of 'Cover-up, cover-up – tell us about the cover-up, pigs!' And 'You tell 'em!' Or 'Yeah, look after your own.' And even, 'Don't let them get away with it!' Kennedy checked to see if there were any Edgar Broughton Band posters about the flat. The next thing he was expecting was chants of 'Out, demons out!' Fortunately, there were only the three people in the room and Jackson's approach was falling somewhat flat.

Kennedy tried again. 'William, I need to know what you were doing on Tuesday 2nd February between the hours 6am and 8am.'

'Do you? Do you, indeed? Well, you're the fuzz so bloody find out. And while you're about it, find out what happened to Susanne Collins. Yes – find out who was where and doing what to whom between the hours of 4pm and 6pm on Friday 22nd January. Yes, find *that* out...' His speech slowed. 'Yes, she's dead. She went into that hospital healthy. We were going to be married, you know? She went into that hospital happy and she never... she never came out.'

Obviously, the thing that William Jackson had spent the last few days hiding away in his subconscious was rising to the surface – and fast. Before long he was sobbing quietly. Kennedy had noticed how glazed his eyes were. Either his doctor – if he had and trusted such a person – had put him on medication or else he was prescribing his own drugs, and not the type you get over the chemist's counter.

Kennedy spoke softly: 'Look, we can talk some other time.'

'Yes,' Irvine added, encouragingly. 'Is there anyone we can get to help you?'

No answer, so Kennedy continued: 'Shall we have a doctor come around? We can radio for one and wait until he arrives.'

'Just get out! That's what you can do , just get out! Just leave me alone! Leave me alone! Oh, God, she was so beautiful and we were going to be married. She didn't do anything wrong, she never did anything wrong. She didn't deserve to die. You wouldn't understand, would you? You're on their side. Just get out – just get out *now*!'

The doorbell rang again, interrupting his tirade. Kennedy hoped that it would be a friend and that they could leave the poor man in safe hands. He was rewarded by the appearance, a few minutes later, by one of Jackson's teaching colleagues.

The teacher, Trevor Davies, at first seemed nervous of the two policemen. He probably thought they were there to arrest Jackson. He quickly regained his composure and attempted to take charge of the situation, ascertaining why they were there. Given his traditional dress-sense and attitude, Davies seemed more of a typical teacher to Kennedy, who was happy to leave Jackson in his care.

Leaving Jackson quietly sobbing in the living-room, the three men walked to the door. 'Look,' said Kennedy, 'he's in too bad a state to continue with our questioning today, we'll have to come back some other time. Do you know what he's on?'

Davies did know what his colleague was on but he was not about to admit it to Kennedy.

Finding no response, Kennedy continued, 'Well, it doesn't matter to me, but to be able to deal with his loss he needs to get off whatever it is, and he needs to get off it soon, otherwise, he'll be another casualty. I don't know exactly what you are to Mr Jackson, but I hope you're a friend. Right now, that's what he needs more than anything.'

'I'll look after him – don't worry,' Davies assured Kennedy.

'I do need to ask him a few more questions and I need to do it as soon as possible. Here's my number,' Kennedy said, writing his name and number on a clean page and tearing it from his book. 'Give me a call when you think he's in a fit state to deal with it. Okay?'

Davies took the piece of paper in silence and closed the door after the two policemen, noticing that one of them was clenching and unclenching his left hand as he walked away.

Chapter Twenty

'Right,' said Kennedy, either to himself or to the wall – it was hard to know which – 'Let's see what we've got here?' After a few minutes silence, he repeated his query. 'What *have* we got here?' A few more moments' thought. 'Nothing,' he replied to the wall and to himself. Surprisingly enough, he didn't feel down or depressed about his lack of progress on the case.

He was becoming more and more convinced that Berry had not committed suicide. Unfortunately, all his leads, if you could call them leads, were turning up blanks.

Irvine had interviewed Berry's solicitor. John Chappell had turned out to be the old small-village style of solicitor, but unfortunately didn't seem to have any especially useful information to give. Berry had been a client for seven years and had contacted him to arrange a meeting for as soon as possible. 'Oh, just a matter I need some information and advice on. We'll discuss it when I come in,' had been Berry's reply when asked what the meeting was for.

'No, he didn't seem unduly worried – more distracted.'

'No, he didn't have any major problems, financial or otherwise.'

'No, I don't think Berry was capable of suicide and I do not think that he committed suicide.'

'No, he didn't come in to see me often – rarely in fact.'

These were among the answers Chappell had supplied to Irvine's questions.

The additional visit to question Martin Shaw and Junior had failed to turn up anything new.

Staff Nurse Rose Butler had been kind enough to furnish Kennedy with the doctor's rosters for the month preceding the death. The sole information the rosters provided was that Dr Burgess had gone off-duty at 1pm on the day of Dr Berry's last shift. He next went on duty at six o'clock the morning Berry drowned.

So, in a way, Kennedy was making some kind of progress. He knew that Dr Burgess could not have murdered Dr Berry. He had an alibi. Alibi is a Latin word meaning 'elsewhere', and when Berry was dropped into Regent's Canal at Cumberland Basin, Burgess had been elsewhere. In fact he had been on duty in front of several witnesses three-and-a-half miles away at All Saints Hospital.

Kennedy found this disappointing in a way because Burgess

would have made a good suspect. Kennedy found that it was always best not to like your suspects, not to feel any sympathy for them.

He flicked through the remainder of the rosters. Nothing caught his eye, so he replaced them in an ever-growing file marked Cumberland Basin Drowning – the name the *Camden News Journal* had given the case.

Superintendent Castle stuck his head around the door. 'Any progress on the Berry thing, yet?'

'No, sir – nothing yet.'

'Ah well, keep at it.' And he was off in a flash, gone about his other business.

How unlike TV cops, Kennedy thought. By this stage, I'd have been carpeted several times and received the usual, We need a breakthrough, we need to give the press something. Not to mention the verbal about budgets, public opinion and promotion – and not necessarily in that order. Scriptwriter's fancy.

It was time to return to the hospital to see Alexander Bowles – the hospital manager – to try and find out more about the Collins patient. It was a meeting Bowles had seemed reluctant to make but eventually he had conceded to Kennedy's polite persistence. Kennedy even had a hard job contacting Bowles by phone. 'He keeps gentleman's hours,' Rose Butler had told Kennedy when he was trying to find out when Bowles would be in his office. 'He gets in at the crack of lunchtime!' she had laughed down the phone.

For someone who didn't drive and would probably never drive, Kennedy was very mobile around London. He loved to walk – great thinking time, he'd explain to those concerned about his lack of personal transport. He travelled on buses and occasionally on the Underground. In an emergency, the Tube was still the quickest way around town, police alarms and flashing lights or not.

Kennedy was always saying to anyone who would listen that by the year 2001 the road system would be full and at a complete and permanent standstill. When that time came, he wanted to be able to know his way around.

He was great at cadging lifts with his colleagues: 'Where are you going to? Oh, great – you can drop me at so-and-so. It's on the way,' was his usual trap.

Today his luck had run out so he chose to walk the fair distance over to St Pancras All Saints Hospital. The walk cleared his head, though he was ready for the cup of tea Alexander 'Call me Alex' Bowles offered at the start of their meeting.

'I suppose you need to know about the Susanne Collins case,' Bowles began.

Kennedy could tell immediately that Bowles was a person who knew how to 'deal' with other people. In fact, he'd made a profession out of it. The problem was that one always felt one was being 'dealt' with.

'I suppose I do,' answered Kennedy.

Bowles consulted his file and he spread several pages out in front of him across the desk. He clasped his hands in front of himself, slightly lower than his cheek. He was ready to speak – Kennedy could tell. 'At 1.10pm on Wednesday 20th January, Ms Susanne Collins was admitted to our emergency unit. The case notes made by the duty-nurse state that Ms Collins had fallen in her school playground and when she tried to rise she found that her leg would not take her weight. Her leg was causing her a great deal of discomfort. Her vitals were all normal...'

'What exactly does that mean?' interrupted Kennedy.

Annoyed that he had been cut off mid-flow and that he was obviously having to address a lay person, Bowles sucked in his breath, not a lot, but enough to be noticeable. 'Her temperature, blood pressure, pulse and breathing – all normal.'

Kennedy realised what was coming so he started to take notes.

'She was running a slight temperature and was still having difficulty standing on her leg. The doctor diagnosed Phlebitis.'

Bowles helpfully spelled it out for Kennedy, before continuing. 'This is an inflammation of the veins and the doctor decided to put her on antibiotics, Ampicillin.' Again, he spelled the word for Kennedy. 'Four injections a day, one every four hours. The doctor decided to admit Ms Collins for observation and to ensure that she would rest and keep her weight off her leg so as to enable the swelling to go down. It's quite incredible how patients, once they know the extent of their ailments, become rather careless. It's when they do not know what the matter with them is that they are more careful and attentive.'

Kennedy nodded, not so much in agreement as in encouragement for Bowles.

'The following day, the 21st, the patient was again attended by the same doctor. The notes state that the swelling had not contracted so he continued with the same dosage of Ampicillin – A–M–P...'

'I–C–I–L–L–I–N. I managed that one, thanks.' This man was bringing out the worst in Kennedy.

'Good. The patient seemed to be in good spirits apart from her slight discomfort. The following afternoon, Friday 22nd, the patient started to become short of breath, nothing serious, and the nurses tried to make her more comfortable. In the early evening, she started to complain about a pain in her chest and was having more trouble breathing. Dr Berry decided to give her a Diamorphine injection to ease the pain.'

Again, Bowles helped Kennedy with his spelling.

'Dr Berry stayed in attendance and, on further examination, realised that Ms Collins was not, in fact, suffering from Phlebitis. He then correctly diagnosed that she had a blood clot which, by this time, had travelled from the leg into her lung. This was what had been causing her shortness of breath and chest pain. Shortly afterwards, Ms Collins lost consciousness. Dr Berry immediately put her on Heparin, H–E–P–A–R–I–N, a drip of ten milligrams to dissolve the clot. Unfortunately, this treatment was too late and the patient expired at 6.23pm on Friday 22nd January.'

Bowles' report was at an end. He turned to Kennedy: 'Your questions, Inspector Kennedy.'

Chapter Twenty-one

'Okay, sir – now correct me if I'm wrong but are you telling me that Ms Susanne Collins died in your hospital because the doctor made the wrong diagnosis?'

'Inspector, I have given you all the facts.'

Alexander Bowles was now doing his schoolteacher bit on Kennedy, who was thinking his remark somewhat evasive.

'Mr Bowles, when this poor woman was admitted to this hospital, did she in fact have a blood clot in her leg?'

'That is a possibility.'

'So, if Susanne Collins' ailment had been correctly diagnosed at the time that she was admitted and she'd been treated with–' he checked his notes – 'with Heparin, then the blood clot would have dissolved before moving to her lung and she would not have died?'

'That is, of course a possibility.'

'Then surely, sir, the hospital trust could now be sued for negligence by Ms Collins' family?'

'Inspector, you are from the police and I have given you the facts. I have told you the truth. I have given you the results of my investigation. I cannot and will not speculate beyond that.'

Christy Kennedy drew in his breath. He was surprised – gobsmacked, even – at what Bowles had just openly admitted to him. 'Have the relatives been given this information, yet?' Kennedy asked quietly.

'No, Inspector – the hospital board have not yet decided on what course of action to take. I have only just concluded my investigation. I would appreciate it very much if you would not make any of this information public.'

Before Kennedy could respond, Bowles added, 'However, if you find yourself in a position where you have to disclose this information, could you please advise me in advance. I imagine the board would wish for Ms Collins' family to be among the first to receive the information. Mr Collins has been causing quite a bit of trouble and has only really quietened down since Dr Berry drowned but I imagine the results of my investigation will have him back on our doorstep again.'

'I imagine it will,' Kennedy stated quietly.

Bowles rose from his chair. 'And if that is all, Inspector?' He offered Kennedy his hand.

Kennedy left the office feeling that he had been 'dealt with'. To Bowles and his precious hospital board, the death of Susanne Collins was just another of their daily problems. Something like raising funds for new equipment or handling complaints from doctors and nurses about their hours and wages. Something like doctors – Burgess, for instance – being unhappy with their parking spaces. Rose Butler had told Kennedy about that one. Or something like keeping the board off his back about overspending.

Kennedy imagined that the minute he left the office, Bowles had closed the Susanne Collins file and had emptied the details of it from his mind.

Here was the death of a young woman – genuinely in the prime of her life – and because of a faulty diagnosis, she was dead. To Alexander Bowles, she was obviously an acceptable loss and his job was to minimise the hospital's exposure on this loss. Bowles was selected for this job not on the strength of his qualities but for his faults.

Chapter Twenty-two

'I can't believe how wrong I was, I just can't believe it.' Kennedy is in his kitchen, sitting at his well-worn farmhouse dining-table, addressing himself to ann rea. It is a large table, but unlike the Berry household dining-table, it's busy – but busy in an orderly way. Everything is set in its own space, as if there were invisible partitions keeping each item in place.

Kennedy has just brewed up one of his special cups of tea and is so preoccupied with his mistake that he fails to realise the significance – if, indeed, there is any – of ann rea being alone with him in his house for the first time.

'I can't believe how stupid I've been – the obvious is usually the truth. Sometimes, it's so simple but we search for something complicated. I nearly fell off the chair when he just came right out and told me the whole story – just, "Blah, blah, blah and then the patient expired. Any questions?" It's totally preposterous,' Kennedy exclaimed.

ann rea sat silently drinking her tea, absorbing his words and home. This man's kitchen was incredibly homely and warm, not at all what she would have expected in a bachelor's home. Perhaps her intuition was correct – perhaps Kennedy was not the usual… but… but she had been here too many times before. She had been hurt too much.

'It's simple,' continued Kennedy, 'Berry made a wrong diagnosis, gave the wrong medication, the patient died, he felt shit about it. Just think about it: he'd let down a patient, his profession, his wife, his son, his calling. He couldn't live with it. That was my mistake, I overlooked his motive for suicide. He was such a highly principled man that he just couldn't take it; he couldn't live with that guilt. He was going to see his solicitor to change his will because he became unbearably depressed about the whole incident and about his life. All his training, all that time studying to reach a peak, and then, with all of that, he still kills a patient. That's probably how he saw it; he probably thought that he'd killed her. Good heavens, it was an accident. He should have talked it over with his wife. But he loved her so much that he couldn't share it with her. He didn't realise that it was exactly because they loved each other so much that they could have shared it. Sheila Berry is strong enough, she could have helped him through this. But he broke the norm – he became drunk, went over to the canal to forget his troubles, decided to end it all and jumped in. Maybe he was so drunk he fell in by accident. Either way he drowned. And I couldn't see it. I was too busy building up this shrine to this great guy and all the time it turns out he's like the rest of us: human. He read the medical situation incorrectly, gave the wrong medicine and the patient died.'

'A sin of omission' ann rea said quietly.

'Pardon?'

'A sin of omission,' she replied. 'It's an American phrase. It's when a doctor, while carrying out his duty, omits to give the correct medication and, as a result, the patient dies. A sin of omission. And then the suing begins. Will the hospital accept liability in this case, Kennedy?'

'Well, I think they're expecting a stink from the brother, but I also think that they're ready to pay out some money. The only question is how much.'

By this time they had both finished their cups of tea so Kennedy had another idea. 'Fancy a glass of wine?'

'Good idea. Shall we go to The Queens?' answered ann rea.

'You mean Pub Schizo?' he replied

'Pardon?'

'You know – the sign outside the pub?'

'What – The Queens?' She didn't have a clue what he was on about.

'Yes – but if you look closely at the sign there's a different queen's head on each side – Queen Alexandra on the Primrose Hill side and Queen Victoria as a young woman on the reverse. So the regulars call it Pub Schizo.'

She laughed with him, as much at his sense of fun as at what he'd just said.

'How about we stay here? I have some cold, crisp Chablis somewhere,' Kennedy suggested.

'Oh, go on, you've twisted my arm. Can I use your loo, though?'

'Of course. First door at the top of the stairs.'

Kennedy opened the wine in her absence and had two glasses poured by the time she returned.

'Your health,' he toasted.

'And yours,' she replied. 'Here's to the end of another case.'

'Looks like it,' he replied.

He was relieved the wine tasted as great as he had remembered. Kennedy quite liked wine but he seemed to sample as much bad wines as good, so he usually forgot the good ones. But on this occasion, luck was with him.

'Great wine, Kennedy!' she said.

ann rea was thinking that she had never seen him as relaxed as this. Was it because of the end of the case or was it because they were becoming more comfortable in each other's company?

Kennedy seemed to like her. The journalist angle didn't seem to put him off. In fact, they had nearly kissed, once. What was I thinking about ann rea asked herself. I nearly let it happen and then I'm in deep shit again. But he's not your regular type of guy, if such a creature does exist. And he's a policeman, for God's sake, but a nice man. But then she thought that they were all nice men when they were trying to do a number on you. It's afterwards that they show their true colours. Been there, done that, didn't like it – next please, ann rea thought as she continued to enjoy the wine.

'So tell me about your writing?' he started.

'What?'

'Your writing – I mean, do you want to be a writer? Books, stories, poetry or whatever. Or are you using this route to break into television, or what?'

'I think out of your list I would probably go for "or what",' she smiled.

'Ah, come on.'

'I'm sorry, Kennedy. I don't really know, is the correct answer. I mean, everyone wants to write the novel. Few do and the majority of those who manage it do so when they're a lot older than I am now. So there must be some kind of sign there. I've tried poetry. I'll have all the words and thoughts and feelings in my head and they'll all sound great – no, not great – more like brilliant, powerful, painful, gentle, dramatic, elegant, playful, happy and sad, but when they spill on to the page, they all sound so… so inarticulate. I suppose I'm in a "look-and-see phase". I don't really know what I want to do with my life eventually. I quite enjoy what I'm doing at the moment and I'm convinced that in time, all will be revealed and I'll realise what I have to do and what I've been waiting around to do.'

'That sounds reasonable to me,' Kennedy ventured.

'Now, in the meantime, Kennedy, I hate to throw a spanner in the works but I have another angle on your Berry/Cumberland Basin case,' ann rea said, shifting the attention from herself.

'A-ha?' said Kennedy, shifting the gears of his brain while thinking that she may be trying to swing the conversation around to a semi-professional level.

'How about… how about if either of the relations, or even both of the relations – brother and boyfriend – have found out, or are suspecting, what you've just told me and they, either separately or together, decide to seek their revenge by kidnapping Berry and dumping him in the canal?'

'Nah. I don't think so. The boyfriend is very upset but he's doomed to be no more than an extra in a documentary. He wouldn't have the guts to do something like that,' Kennedy replied.

'But perhaps he's in his current state precisely because he killed Berry?' suggested ann rea.

'Hmm.'

Kennedy sipped more wine.

ann rea continued further along this line of thought. 'He – or the both of them – did it in a way that made it look like Berry committed suicide.'

'Well…' You could see the wheels of his brain slowly begin to turn again. Bowles did say that the brother was becoming quite trouble-some and Rose Butler told me of a violent scene the brother had at the hospital. But then they, or one of them, would almost certainly have been spotted by the Boat People.'

'The Boat People?' queried ann rea.

'In the office, Martin Shaw and Junior have become known as the Boat People.'

'Ah, but you're assuming that the splash that these so-called Boat People heard was in fact Berry jumping or being pushed into the canal. But if this wasn't the case and Berry jumped – or was pushed – into the canal before or after the Boat People left, then the Boat People would not necessarily have seen the person or persons who pushed him in. And that person or persons, your honour, could be… could in fact be the brother and/or the boyfriend.'

ann rea was obviously enjoying herself, and Kennedy thought she might even be on the right track.

'In fact,' she continued, 'they could have been waiting in the bushes until the boat had pulled out or cast off, or whatever they call it. There are bushes there Kennedy, are there not, bushes to suit my case?'

'No.' He considered the scene again in his mind's eye. 'Just a locked-up hut, a high fence and… you're right, you know… good God, you're right!' Kennedy cried.

'I'm right? Who killed Berry? Who… the brother? The boyfriend? Who Kennedy? Hello – Kennedy?' ann rea demanded from the wall of thought.

'I missed it, I missed it. Berry did not commit suicide and he didn't fall into the canal by accident, or indeed on purpose. Come on, ann rea, grab your coat. I'll show you what I mean. Come on!'

'My wine, my wine, Kennedy. I was enjoying it!'

Too late. He was in the hall on the way out of the house and unless she followed him, and pretty damn quick at that, chances are she would never know what this Detective Inspector Christy Kennedy was on about.

'Wait for me, Kennedy, wait for me. I'm coming.'

ann rea took a quick slug of wine, put on her coat and scarf, grabbed her bag and ran after him in the time it had taken another Christie to win the Olympic Gold for the 100 metres.

Chapter Twenty-three

'Look! There!' Kennedy pointed. They had half-run, half-walked the mile or so to the Cumberland Basin. The heavy rain had ceased, unveiling a full moon. From one side, the moon lit the bridge they were standing on whilst the lights from the Feng Shang floating restaurant illuminated the other.

It was obvious from Kennedy's agitation that he had stumbled upon something important to the case. Just exactly what that was remained a mystery to ann rea.

'What's going on? What is it Kennedy?' she asked again.

'Okay. The only way it's possible to be on that bank of the canal,' he started, pointing to the zoo bank, directly opposite the Feng Shang, 'is if you come down there by the side entrance – near the zoo building, down the steep bank and through that gate. That's a very high fence, with barbed wire on top, so there's no other way down.'

'So?' ann rea inquired, still not following him.

'Now, that gate remains locked until Junior opens it first thing in the morning and he arrives around six-thirty. He spends some time preparing the boat and awaiting the arrival of his work mate, Martin Shaw. The gate is locked after them. That side is not open to the public – boat-owners only. The public walkway is on the other side. This side dead-ends up there at the top of the basin. The public side…' he turned and pointed to the other side, 'continues around under that bridge and heads up towards Camden Lock. So that means that Berry could not have reached the bank by accident. He could not have made his own way there to jump or fall in.'

'Couldn't he just have jumped from up here on the bridge?' ann rea asked.

'No, impossible. His body was found over there, you see? Where the Sailing Diamond is moored now – that must be at least twenty feet away. It would be impossible to jump so far,' answered Kennedy.

'What if he jumped down on to the bank and then made his way to the point where he leapt in?'

'Well, to jump that distance on to a hard surface, he'd have broken some bones, and a doctor would certainly have known that, plus there would have been some marks or swelling on his body as a result. Berry had no such marks or broken bones when he was found,' Kennedy said, triggering off another of his thoughts. 'Ah! No marks, except the faint line along the front of his chest, underarm to underarm. That would explain that,' Kennedy said, racing ahead again.

'Pardon? Please explain what you're on about now. I'm beginning to think I shouldn't have had that wine, Kennedy.'

'Okay. At first we thought the mark across Dr Berry's chest was caused by his clothes hunching up under his arms and pulling tight when he was pulled out of the water. But it would make a lot more sense…' this time ann rea waited for the explanation, 'if someone had tied a rope around him – under the arms – and lowered him over the side of the bridge down on to the bank.'

'Wouldn't that be rather awkward to achieve?'

'Not really. You'd rest the body on the railing, here; lean the body over; place the rope around this knob, here; let the body slide gently over. The rope on the knob would take the strain. After that, it wouldn't be difficult to lower the body down on to the bank. If someone was reasonably strong it would be do-able.'

Kennedy walked to and fro the length of the isolated bridge, checking angles, heights, weighing up possibilities. He had formed his theory as to the disposal of the body and was now checking to see if anything could disprove his hypothesis.

'Yes, yes, yes!' cried Kennedy, in a rare burst of excitement.

'This is the most excited I've ever seen anyone get without taking their clothes off,' smiled ann rea.

'Sorry, it's just that I wasn't sure. I thought that he didn't or wouldn't commit suicide. I had that feeling but I couldn't find anything to convince me either way. Then, Alexander "Call me bleedin' Alex" Bowles' statement made it plausible that Berry could indeed have committed suicide. Berry had made a critical mistake and a patient had died as a result. I was beginning to think that maybe when he was feeling very down about it he just might… just might have taken his own life. But this – this fence – proves that Berry was brought here by a second party who wanted to do him harm.'

'So, Kennedy, now you've proved to me that you're a genius, my big question is, who killed Berry?'

'Ha, that's a good one. Too early to say yet. But now that I know it was murder, it'll be easier to proceed from here.'

'How?'

'Well, I'll have to re-interview a few people, taking this new information into consideration. And I've still a couple of people to talk to, yet. But this is important.'

Kennedy continued to survey the scene. ann rea was tired. 'Sorry, Kennedy, it's late. Don't forget I'm a working girl. I'll walk you back to your house – I've left my car just around the corner.'

They walked off into the night, arm in arm. To strangers, they looked like lovers, but Kennedy felt this relationship, though growing stronger, was still not heading in the romantic direction he wished for it.

'What was that bit in your column this week about Nigel Mansell? I saw the picture and the headline but I didn't get a chance to read it,' he asked, as they crossed the moonlit Primrose Hill.

'Oh, that,' laughed ann rea. 'Well, apparently, last season after one of the time trials, Mansell stormed into the pits telling his mechanics that he needed more power. One of the mechanics answered, "Sorry Nigel – it's going flat out. There's nothing else to give." Nigel wasn't satisfied, he wanted to go faster. "There must be something you can do to make me go faster," the brummie pleaded. "Well, Nigel," one of the mechanics answered, looking at Mansell's well-filled driving suit, "Perhaps if you were to lose a little weight, that would speed things up a bit." Mansell left the pits, only to return twenty minutes later, minus his famous moustache, announcing to the mechanics, "Okay, I've done my bit. I've lost some weight. Now it's your turn – make me go faster."'

'Is that true?' laughed Kennedy.

'It's supposed to be. Anyway, Kennedy, here we are.'

ann rea took out the keys to her car and glanced at him. They were both silent. A lorry came noisily around the corner and broke the trance. ann rea got into her snazzy maroon saloon, a vintage Ford Popular, started the engine and waved goodbye. As she pulled away, she could see Kennedy in her rear-view mirror staring after her. If she could have read his thoughts, she'd have heard him think, One step forward and two steps back. And he wasn't thinking about the Berry case.

That was for tomorrow.

Chapter Twenty-four

Kennedy walked to his office the next morning with an inch to his step. He immediately summoned Irvine and instructed him to assemble the team – small though it was – to meet in his office in twenty minutes' time. The twenty minutes, Kennedy hoped, would be enough to bring Castle up to date on the case. Kennedy also needed Castle's approval for his next step.

Running through the previous evening's events took longer than he thought it would. He was prepared to spend extra time 'selling' his theory to Superintendent Castle. As it happened, Castle took little persuading.

'That seems fine to me, Kennedy,' he said at length. 'Please proceed as you see fit and keep me appraised of your progress.'

The superintendent was happy that Kennedy now had a handle on the case. Yesterday, he had felt the case was losing momentum and would probably end up in the growing 'unsolved cases' pile.

Kennedy was fired up and raring to go.

'Right,' he began, addressing the team in his office. 'I think it;s pretty safe to assume that this is now a murder case. Superintendent Castle and I are convinced that Edmund Berry did not take his own life.'

Kennedy explained in detail his discoveries of the previous evening. There were questions similar to those of ann rea and he gave similar answers.

'Okay, friends – we've been letting the trail grow cold so now's the time for each of us to get back into this in a big way. Here's what I want…'

Kennedy held up his left hand and moved his fingers through the points as he called them out.

'…One – DS Irvine – call forensic out and have them check all those knobbly things on the bridge to see if a rope was used to lower a heavy load.'

'Right, sir,' answered Irvine.

'Two…' Kennedy was still looking at Irvine – 'Find out from Trevor Davies…' Irvine looked blank. 'You know, that friend of William Jackson's. Find out how whether Jackson had told him that he specifically blamed Berry for the death of Susanne Collins, and if Davies knows what Jackson was doing between 5am and 8am on the morning Berry was murdered. And try get as much background as you can on Jackson.'

'Three…' Kennedy addressed himself to DC Milligan. '…I want you to go back to Cumberland Basin and join Martin Shaw and Junior on one of their trips. Observe everything that goes on. Get there first thing in the morning, early, around 5am. Hang around. See what happens at that time of the morning. See who's out and about then. If you meet anyone, stop them, question them, see if they're regulars. See if they remember anything at all about the morning in question. Be ready when the Sailing Diamond casts off. Stand on the boat's roof and look backwards and find out if it's possible to see back to the bank. Have Martin Shaw tell you at what point on the journey he heard the splash, look around then and see what's visible on the bank. I don't know what you're after – it doesn't matter – just bring me back anything, anything at all.'

Milligan beamed from ear to ear, It was a chance to prove himself and he was determined not to let the DI down. He was determined to find something of relevance.

Kennedy unleashed another finger – his fourth – and now all were taut and outstretched, like the tail feathers of a dove pigeon. He stared at Constable Lundy – a bit of a yuppie cop, with the hair style but not the income to match.

'Four. I want you, Lundy, to contact *Crime Watch*, Greater London Radio, Capital Radio, *Evening Standard*, and *Camden News Journal*.'

'Radio One, sir?' inquired Lundy.

'No, don't bother, no one listens to them any more…' A couple of officers picked up on Kennedy's joke and laughed, '…Ask that all of them put out the story. Between the hours of five o'clock and eight o'clock on the morning of Tuesday 2nd February, a body was dumped into Regent's Canal at the Cumberland Basin. The police are looking for people who may have seen anything suspicious at that time. The usual "all calls will be treated in confidence". The desk-sergeant will help you out with the exact wording. I don't care how insignificant these people feel their information is, I want to hear it and the sooner I hear it, the better.' Lundy noted Kennedy's requirements.

'And five…' Kennedy's thumb came up and he smiled at WPC Coles, '…I want you to visit Primrose Hill Primary School. Find out all you can – gossip, everything you can – about William Jackson and Susanne Collins. Again, same as DS Irvine, dig up all you can about William Jackson. You know what I want. What kind of a person is he? Were they in love? Did he love her enough to kill for her? Did she see other men? Did he see other women? Was he possessive? Was she possessive? Again, try to find out if anyone has any idea about what Jackson was doing on the morning Berry was murdered. You and DS

Irvine should then compare notes and do any cross-checking on alibis, locations, etc.'

Kennedy seemed happy with his strategy. 'And that is the end of my fingers.' They all stare at him. 'But, of course, there's me. I nearly forgot about myself. Well, when you're off doing all the hard work, I'll be spending an hour and fifty-one minutes with The Beatles.'

They grunted and groaned but knew better than to voice complaints.

'That's it, go to it. Let's go out and find who did it.' And then, as an afterthought, Kennedy added, 'And let's be careful out there.'

They all laughed as they disbanded.

Chapter Twenty-five

An hour and fifty-one minutes is the time it takes to get by train from Euston to Derby. The time passes quicker with *A Hard Day's Night* and *Revolver* on your Walkman, as Kennedy found out that journey. After having listened to the Fab Four for nearly three decades, he still found it hard to believe how brilliant a band they were and how much pleasure they had given him. Songs like 'And I Love Her', 'If I fell' and 'I Should Have Known Better' are truly magic. When something's as wonderful as that you try hard to analyse it – to work out why the music moves you so much. The secret, if there is one, is in the simplicity. It seemed fitting to Kennedy, as he travelled deeper and deeper into the pure English countryside, that he should be listening to England's finest folk music from England's finest folk group.

The stations rolled by his window – Bedford, Wellingborough, Kettering, Market Harborough and Leicester. The Beatle melodies rolled around his head.

Kennedy was happy to be out of London for a spell. He'd always loved train journeys as a child and it was a passion he had maintained into adulthood. Apart from anything else, you get a chance to look into backyards. Back gardens are so different to front gardens. A front garden is a showpiece, where everything is in its correct place for the world to see. Backyards give a truer picture of the household's inhabitants: the way people leave things they feel are not in public view.

Kennedy wondered what Norman Collins' backyard might say about Norman Collins that perhaps Norman Collins might not say about himself.

'Good old Tim O'Flynn,' Kennedy muttered to himself as he noticed a member of the local plod waiting for him at the ticket barrier. Camden's finest desk-sergeant – the cunning, white-haired Timothy O'Flynn – had promised to have someone meet Kennedy at the station and ease his way around Derby. Funny, thought Kennedy, you can always spot the local constabulary. He wondered if he was as noticeable in London.

'Constable Harold Black at your service, sir. Welcome to Derby.'

The local bobby greeted Kennedy just as he was thinking that Derby was a funny kind of city – not far enough south to be southern and not spunky enough to be a Birmingham, Liverpool or Newcastle.

'Thank you, Constable – thanks for meeting me.' Kennedy shook the other's hand before they pushed their way through the throng to the station car-park.

'Now, sir, how do you feel after your journey?' inquired the constable as they climbed into the unmarked police car. Without giving Kennedy a chance to answer, he posed a second question. 'Fancy a quick lunch before we head out to the Collins' neck of the woods? I know a great little pub, The Mucky Duck, it's just off the Mansfield Road, on our route. They do a choice pub lunch.'

'Sounds great to me, Constable – lead on,' said Kennedy, as they hit the road. No clouds of dust or New York-style burning rubber here, just a conservative and unremarkable commencement to their journey.

Kennedy flashed through the radio tuner in the hope of finding something local to tune into. Having no success, he gave up.

'So, Constable Black, what do you know about this Collins' family?'

'Well, sir,' he began, as they passed the police station in Full Street, 'Norman Collins is forty-six-years-old. He's lived in Derby all his life as has his father, Tom Collins, who resides in Lodge Lane in the north-west of the city. Norman is married with two teenage children – one boy, called Tom, after his grandad, and a daughter, Geraldine. Norman works as a railway ticket clerk. He's an ardent pigeon-fancier and he's never been in trouble. It's a very close-knit family and from what we hear, the father's not been the same since Susanne's death. Apparently, he just mopes around all day as if he's given up. Norman visits him regularly but it seems not a word passes between them.'

'I'm impressed,' said Kennedy. 'How on earth did you manage to find all this out?'

'Ah, sir – inside information. The wife's sister does the local meals-on-wheels and Tom Collins is one of her stops.'

'I see,' said Kennedy, as they pulled into the car-park of The Black Swan. 'I assume this is the establishment for lunch?'

Chapter Twenty-six

Constable Black had not been wrong – the lunch was excellent and the *craic*, as Kennedy's mother would say, was 'ninety'. Harold took a liking to Kennedy, 'Even though you work in London,' as he put it – and Kennedy appreciated the other's northern humour.

'What's the difference between Manchester United and an arsonist?' he asked Kennedy.

'Give up,' replied Kennedy.

'An arsonist wouldn't throw away his last three matches,' joked Black.

After lunch, they drove back down the Mansfield Road, the A61, for about five minutes, before pulling into Handyside Street. The Collins' residence was semi-detached and backed on to school playing fields.

Black anticipated Kennedy's thoughts. 'He's expecting us; he took the afternoon off work.'

The house was small and nothing fancy but clean and very cosy. The minute the door opened, Kennedy's nostrils were tickled deliciously with the smells of home-baked bread. The house was very 'lived-in' and had a comfortable air about it. It is what is classed a 'functional' as opposed to a 'beautiful' house.

Kennedy was somewhat surprised by the welcome he received. He was more used to people resenting his presence in their homes and could always sense their impatience to get rid of him. But Norman Collins shook his hand very firmly and bade him enter. Out of the corner of his eye, Kennedy noticed the woman of the house slip off her apron and hide it under one of the cushions scattered on the living-room sofa.

'This is the wife,' announced Norman. 'Come on through.'

They were shown to the living-room. The room was warm (very warm) from a heartily burning coal fire. Kennedy was invited to take off his coat and did so. He sat down on the sofa and sank down and then down further for what seemed like ages. He could imagine sinking into it after the Sunday lunch and just drifting off – in and out of consciousness. It was not your high-street furniture-store sofa, but part of a genuine farmhouse suite. The chair to the right of the settee was obviously 'dad's chair', with all his bits close to hand – slippers, pipe, tobacco, matches, ashtray, newspaper, reading glasses and dog, Jonesy.

The television was perched in the corner so all seats in the room had a view of it. There was a large wooden cupboard decked out with various ornaments. One shelf seemed to be reserved for trophies. At first Kennedy thought they were for darts but on closer inspection he saw they were prizes for pigeon racing and showing.

The walls were sparsely covered, with some family pictures and a couple of paintings of countryside scenes. But the biggest surprise awaiting Kennedy was directly above the fireplace. Taking off towards heaven were three flying ducks. Kennedy had never seen a set in real life before – only on television, where they had decorated the wall above Stan and Hilda Ogden's fireplace for twelve years.

'Fancy a cup of tea, lad?' offered Norman.

Kennedy wanted a chance to move out of the sitting-room because he felt their conversation would be too formal.

'Yes, great idea. Let's have a cup of tea in the kitchen,' he said.

Norman Collins smiled.

This is better, Kennedy thought to himself as they settled around the kitchen dining-table, much better in here. He could see that Mrs Collins was slightly anxious about their new location, which he put down to a touch of the front-garden/back-garden factor.

Anyway, she made an astonishing brew of tea, refreshing yet delicate. Norman was about to help himself to one of the McVities chocolate digestive biscuits from the packet. The packet was sitting in the centre of the table along with the salt, pepper, HP Sauce, Heinz ketchup, a bottle of milk and a sugar bowl. His wife snatched the packet away before you could say 'mushy peas' or even help yourself to one. Before he had a chance to complain, they were returned to the table, only this time neatly displayed on a flowery plate complete with some cheesecakes for good measure.

Unfortunately these home-baked cheesecakes were a favourite of Kennedy's. Mrs Collins' originals were delicious – moreish. Very moreish in fact.

Ten minutes elapsed before Mrs Collins left them in the kitchen, no doubt to reclaim her apron and return to her dusting. The three men sat around the kitchen table. Kennedy had positioned himself so that both the constable and Collins faced him on the other side of the table.

'When did you first hear of Susanne's sickness?' Kennedy began.

'She rang me from the hospital to tell me herself, it was on the Wednesday afternoon, an hour or so after she'd been admitted. You can imagine what I thought, but she quickly explained what had happened. She'd collapsed in the playground... she'd felt this burning pain in her leg. She said it was impossible for her to put any weight on it. Anyway William, William Jackson had turned up at the hospital and she'd asked him to go and ring me and tell me what had happened. She'd planned to tell the nurses not to let him back in again. She was scared that I would be ringing her at her flat and would get worried about her when there was no answer. But Jackson was about as much use to her as a chocolate teapot, he refused to call me. So, when he left, she rang me herself. Said she felt all the better for it, too.'

'How did she sound?'

'She sounded fine, did our Susie. I asked her if she needed me to come down. You see, she'd been planning to come up here for the weekend and I offered to go down and bring her back with me. But she said she'd be okay. She hoped to be out of hospital the next day and she was going to come straight up here, taking the rest of the week off school.'

'Was that a special family weekend or something?' Kennedy asked.

'No, not special, just that Dad had been missing her since she went back to London after the Christmas holidays. She was also trying to split up with Jackson. So, she thought the weekend in Derby would be good for her on both counts.'

'You say she was trying to split up with Jackson?'

'Yes, he wasn't really her type and he had just kind of latched himself on to her, all the time trying to be more to her than he really was. They spent some time together, but our Susie assured me it wasn't serious. At first, she said that she pitied him but lately he'd been getting on her nerves so she had told him – politely at first – that it was over. Or, more correctly, that it was never going to start. But he kept on bugging her – telling everyone that he was her boyfriend. She told him she didn't even want to see him as a friend anymore. She just wanted Jackson out of her life altogether.'

Collins paused and seemed to be thinking about what he was about to say.

'I asked her if she wanted me to come down and warn Jackson off. Our Susie got really mad with me for that, said she was well capable of looking after herself, that she didn't want her big brother coming down and beating up troublesome boyfriends. "That would do my reputation the world of good," she'd said. She told me it was the nineties and people didn't do that anymore, these days women could look after themselves. She was so annoyed with me, she put the phone down. Half an hour later, she rang back to say she was sorry. Jackson was getting her down but she really had to sort it out herself.'

Again, Collins paused; it obviously wasn't easy for him.

'I rang again on Thursday and Friday and on both occasions I was told that she was resting. On the Friday, the doctor also told me that she was "uncomfortable". She was experiencing some difficulties in breathing, so I left work early and caught the next train down to London.'

A few moments of silence passed until he spoke again, this time his eyes filling with tears.

'By the time I reached the hospital, she was dead. They'd let her die, Inspector and she'd been healthy all her life. The apple of the old man's eye. Now she's dead and all the hospital can say is that they're carrying out an investigation. What use is that to us now?'

Norman Collins wiped the tears from his eyes, not embarrassed. 'Are you going to find out what happened to our Susie, sir?'

Kennedy felt awkward. He didn't like to lie just to get information out of a witness. 'Well, actually, I'm working on the mystery surrounding the death of Susanne's doctor at the hospital, a Dr Berry.'

'Oh, him,' was the only reply.

Norman Collins' mood shifted. He pushed back his chair from the table and stood up.

'Time to feed the pigeons.' He put on an old British Rail jacket and a cloth cap, which had been hanging on the back of the door. Along with his blue checked shirt, well-worn brown cords and black, leather boots, he looked like he might be nipping out for a loaf of Hovis. 'Fancy coming with me, Inspector?'

Kennedy nodded positively.

'There'll only be room for the two of us,' said Norman Collins, looking at Constable Black. 'Will you be okay here? Call the missus if you need anything.'

Chapter Twenty-seven

The noise of the pigeons flapping their wings as Kennedy and Norman Collins entered the loft was deafening. 'It's just that there's a stranger in the loft,' he reassured Kennedy. 'Come on, come on,' he said to his birds, quietly persuading them to settle down with gentle words and whistles. 'That's better. Now, when you're totally quiet you'll get your grub,' he smiled.

Collins filled their dishes – cleaned-out Fray Bentos steak and kidney pie tins – with a selection of grains. All the perches seemed to empty at once as the birds alighted on the floor, close to their dishes, and tucked into their dinner.

'She'd come in here with me, our Susie would, and we'd talk a lot. She liked being around the pigeons. We'd talk about everything in here, we would. I liked her, sir, you know, I really liked her. I believe that if she hadn't been my sister we still would have been good friends. She cared about things, you could talk to her.

'That's one of the things I'm still trying to come to terms with,' continued Collins, his voice following the tangent his mind had already set off on. 'You have this wonderful person, you know, okay, I know she was my sister but I still think she was a wonderful person and you think of everything that has gone into her life. All of it – you know, her growing up, our parents clothing her and feeding her, teaching her right and teaching her wrong, sending her to school to learn all the various subjects and also to learn the ways of life. The pain she and my parents felt as she grew up – them watching her walk the tightrope of life hoping that she wouldn't fall off and hurt herself. Her taking step after step up there, hoping her next step would be as sound as her last step but not being entirely sure.'

Collins filled a dish with water for his birds.

'I remember our mother used to take us to the cinema, to the matinee every Saturday, and our Susie would sit quietly watching it, taking it all in, and then, when the film were over and we would be walking home, she'd bombard my mother with hundreds of questions about the movie. "Why did he leave her?" "Why didn't the robbers see that, when they killed the sheriff, the sheriff's baby daughter would have no father?" "Why did the school teacher throw the girl out of class? You saw, Ma – she wasn't the one being naughty – it was that horrible boy behind her?" "Why does Old Mother Riley dress up in women's clothes, everyone can see that he's a man?" And then, after about a dozen questions and answers, they would arrive home. Our mother would make the tea and our Susie would tell me dad all about the film.'

Collins' eyes filled again.

'Later, her dealing with boyfriends and all the pleasure, joys and pains of that. And then the work, the sweat to pass all the exams and each time you think, Great, I've made it now, until someone else comes along and says, Well, you did really well in that exam but that really wasn't the important one. And the same thing happens again, and again. You never get to the point where you let yourself off the hook. You never reach the point where you can say, Okay, I'm here, this is it. It's great here and I'm going to use this time to enjoy it. You're always pushing and pushing to get to somewhere else and you never arrive. And now our Susie is gone and it's all over. That's what I find hard to accept. Why was all that hard work, all that living, why was it all in vain?'

Kennedy said nothing. He felt that Norman was getting something off his chest. Perhaps this was his first opportunity to let it all out.

'Why does someone good and kind like our Susie have to die after going through all of that? Twenty-eight years of hard work, day after day. She never had a bad thought for anyone. Why does she have to lose it all? Why was her life in vain while some of these other totally useless shits, shits whose minds are on other things, get to take her life away and be allowed to live?. Can you tell me why? I can't work it out, I really can't. I know that being a good person is not selfish, being a bad person is pure selfishness. So, how does that add up?'

Kennedy didn't know whether he'd been asked a question or not. It was certainly something he didn't know the answer to.

His mind wandered to Sheila Berry and to her son, Sam, and to how much pain they had been dealt. Yet Kennedy felt that Norman Collins was convinced that Berry was the person responsible for the death of his sister. It was clear that, at this moment, Norman Collins would certainly not have any pity for Berry or for his family.

Kennedy also wondered if the man in front of him, with his prize pigeons, his gentle, caring, loving hands – could this man also have used those caring and loving hands to push Berry into the cold and muddy waters of the Regent's Canal? A canal that was one hundred and twenty-eight and one-half miles away.

The motive was certainly there. The means were there. Few murderers are professionals and execute beautiful jobs. But as for the resolution – Kennedy was not so sure about that – about whether this man had the badness in him to end someone else's life. Even with his belief that Berry's mistake had caused his sister's death, Kennedy didn't know if Norman Collins had that darkness, that badness in him to kill. Kennedy was not convinced that Norman knew as much about the death of his sister as Bowles had admitted in London.

'This one…' Collins broke the silence between them. 'This silver mealy was last year's Penzance young birds winner. Twelve-hundred-and-eight-yards per minute – thirty-four yards per minute faster than the second bird. We've got great hopes for this one this year.'

Collins put the pigeon down.

'But what does it matter? Our Susie used to telephone me after the races to see how the birds did. She was very supportive, you know. When the birds did well, she was real proud and excited and when they didn't do well, she'd come up with all these reasons and excuses. She'd say, rest them up well and they'll do great next time. She'd have these funny excuses, you know, like, "So the silver mealy decided to do a bit of window-shopping," and, "Did it stop off in London on the way home?" Another time, she said, "I saw the silver mealy the last time I was up and she was fighting with her old man. You know – she probably just decided to stay out all night to get her own back on him".'

Kennedy laughed and then said softly, 'That's why you have to keep your energies up. You have to keep Susie's spirit alive.'

'But what about our dad? You can't live a life just for the memories and that's all he has now. All his dreams for her will never be realised. He's just waiting… it looks like he's just waiting to die. And who's responsible for that? Who answers for that, Inspector?'

Collins had picked up another pigeon. Its legs were placed between his first and second fingers so as to allow the thumb to hold the wings in whilst he examined the bird with his other hand. 'Got to make sure that the eyes are clear and that the nose is white,' he said, taking the wing with his free hand and fanning it out. 'You have to make sure that no feathers are missing.'

They both examined the splendid wing. Kennedy was happy that no answer had really been sought for the last unanswered question. The dark clouds hovering above Norman Collins' head seemed to drift slightly away as he became distracted with his pigeons. The outstretched bird's wings revealed its magnificent feathers – functionally arranged by nature to create a light air-sealed propeller.

'Pigeons! You do your best to care for them. Groom them, feed them, train them. Then you let them out into the open air and they lose your protection. Many things can hurt and harm them – telegraph wires, cats, hawks, guns, they can all end these harmless lives in a second. But no matter what you do for them, no matter how much you love them, there's absolutely nothing that you can do to stop them getting hurt.'

Neither spoke for a period – it could have been thirty seconds, it could have been five or six minutes. Neither man was conscious of not speaking. The only sound was the cooing of the pigeons. Kennedy followed their antics as they chased one another around the loft. His thoughts drifted to ann rea.

'We'd better be getting back into the house or she'll be having that poor policeman helping her with the cleaning.'

'Yes, yes,' smiled Kennedy. 'Just one final thing I need to ask before we go in. I need to know where you were late in the evening of Monday 1st February and early morning of Tuesday 2nd of February?'

Norman Collins smiled. 'Well, I might as well tell you 'cause it wouldn't be hard to find out.' He paused as he locked the pigeon grain away.

'Well?' Kennedy said softly, not wishing to distract him from anything he wished to say.

'I was in London.'

Chapter Twenty-eight

A m I about to hear a confession? thought Kennedy.
Out loud he said to Collins: 'You want to tell me about it?
'Well, I caught the 6am train down to St Pancras on the morning of 2nd February.'

'Oh,' said Kennedy, moving slowly from foot to foot as his fingers started to flex.

'I frequently do that when I'm training the pigeons. I get free rail passes and I take the pigeons down to London to release them and then they fly home. London is the furthest distance you can travel to from Derby in the shortest time. When pigeons are young, Inspector, you train them for races by taking them short distances away from the loft. To start with, just before feeding time on their first day's training, you put them all in one of those baskets.'

Collins opened one of the cupboards in the loft to reveal various-sized basketwork containers with small windows around the perimeter.

'You put the pigeons in through this single-size trapdoor in the top of the basket and you release them by this…' he flipped open the basket, 'see, the whole of the top of the basket opens up. So, to start with, I take the pigeons across to the other side of those playing fields over there and release them. They're hungry so they fly directly back here for the grub. After about two or three days of that, I double the distance, release them about two streets away and the same thing, they fly back. Then I strap the basket to the back of my old bike and I'll cycle a mile and let them off, then a mile in a different direction, gradually building the distance up to ten miles. That's when I start to use the train. I take them all over the place and release them and they'll fly home.'

'How do they do that? How do they know how to fly home?' Kennedy inquired.

'Ah, that's a good one, that's a good question, Inspector, and the real answer is that no-one knows. Oh, there are lots of theories about magnetic guides, about the pigeon's picking up the landmarks, that's why a lot of pigeon-fanciers will paint their lofts with bright stripes and so on, so that the pigeon can pick it out as an easy landmark in the rest of the drab countryside. Whatever, they always find their way home and they always do it in pretty quick time. The silver mealy for instance – that race I was telling you about was from a place in France, just over four hundred and sixty miles away and the silver mealy averaged twelve hundred and eight yards per minute for that journey. That's an average speed of just over forty-one miles per hour.'

Kennedy was taking it all in, though he silently communicated that he still needed an answer to his first question.

'Okay, Inspector – on the morning of 2nd February, I arrived at St Pancras at 7.50am, let the pigeons off in Regent's Park at about eight-twenty and caught the nine o'clock back to Derby, arriving at ten-forty-three. I came straight from the station to here and found that the pigeons were already home. The missus made me some lunch and I clocked in at work at one o'clock.'

'Bit of a rush, wasn't it?' suggested Kennedy.

'No, not really – I don't mind travelling by train, particularly during off-peak periods when the carriages aren't packed.' Norman Collins smiled and opened the loft door. 'Shall we join the others, Inspector?'

Chapter Twenty-nine

Kennedy returned to London on the seven o'clock train. He could almost as easily have caught the six o'clock but he figured that it would have been packed with commuters returning from work. Business-hour trains seemed to have become the singles bars of the nineties – he wanted to avoid all that peacock preening. He used the extra hour to pick up a railway timetable, a railway cup of tea (contrary to legend, Kennedy had tasted worse) and two of Mr Kipling's apple pies. Kennedy concurred that Mr Kipling did in fact make exceedingly good cakes.

As he walked through his front door, the grandfather clock in his hallway began chiming nine o'clock. Kennedy wondered how the rest of his team had fared in his absence. The answer to that question would have to wait until morning.

Dialling ann rea's number, he realised that he now knew her well enough to call her up without needing a specific reason.

'Hello.'

'Kennedy.' She seemed happy that he'd phoned.

'How'ya doing?'

'Fine, Kennedy. Where have you been all day? I've been trying to get hold of you.'

'I was in Derby.'

'Seeing who?'

'Seeing Susanne Collins' brother, Norman.'

'Learn anything?'

'I'm not sure.' He thought for a few moments, their ears sharing the same crackle – British Telecom's contribution to the technological revolution of the nineties. 'So, what were you ringing me for then?'

'I was going to invite you around here tonight for dinner, but it's too late now,' replied ann rea.

'Oh,' he muttered, the disappointment evident in his voice.

'You had your chance, Kennedy. I've already eaten, and besides, I'm comfy in bed engrossed in Garrison Keillor's new book. I'm meant to be reviewing it for next week's *Journal*.'

'Oh, well, sorry about that,' said Kennedy dejectedly, blasting Mr Kipling under his breath.

'Come on, Kennedy, there'll be other opportunities.'

'There will?'

'Sure. You and I are going to be friends.'

That reminded Kennedy of his childhood.

'Kennedy? Hello? Are you still there,' ann rea said, chasing away the silence.

'Yes, sorry. It's funny, when you said, "We're going to be friends", it reminded me of when I was a boy. At that age, you could be that direct with people. You're not scared of coming right out and saying, Will you be my friend? And that was it – if you both agreed, you'd be friends. The older you become, the less you deal with things in that direct, honest manner.'

'So, are you going to be my friend, Kennedy?' she said with more than a hint of mocking coyness.

'Yes,' he answered, with absolute certainty.

'Good, that's settled then,' she replied.

'Is that all we're going to be, ann rea?'

'Hmm, you're just going to have to wait and find out, aren't you, Kennedy,' she laughed. 'In the meantime, I'm curling up with Garrison Keillor. Goodnight, Kennedy.'

'Goodnight, ann rea.'

Kennedy wasn't sure if he'd managed to speak the words before she'd disconnected. He felt strangely fulfilled, enlightened. The odd thing was that the more he thought about it, the better he felt about being her friend.

His lasting thought that night was that if they were to become lovers then perhaps they wouldn't be lovers forever, but they'd certainly be friends forever – or, at least, friends for life.

Chapter Thirty

Detective Sergeant Irvine's intercom was buzzing when he walked into his office the next morning at seven-forty-five. 'James – it's Kennedy. Could you round up the posse for a meeting in my room in, say… thirty minutes, eight-fifteen, okay?'

'Righto, sir.'

'Oh, and one other thing – let's pretend we're American and have the desk-sergeant rustle up tea, coffee and doughnuts for the whole team,' added Kennedy.

'You've got it, chief.'

He's certainly in a good mood today, Irvine thought. But now he set himself the task, he couldn't remember the last time Kennedy had been in a bad mood. Nonetheless, he's certainly in a *great* mood today, Irvine concluded as he set off to carry out the colourful request.

Kennedy spent a few minutes updating his noticeboard. He pinned up the Derby–London timetable. He also added Norman Collins' movements to his own case timetable.

Further study of the noticeboard offered up no great revelations to Kennedy. He wondered if any more of the missing links in the case would find their way up on to the board before the end of the meeting.

The team were all greatly amused by the supply of doughnuts. As they tucked in, Kennedy got the ball rolling: 'Okay, let's do an info-check and see if we – any of us, all of us – picked up anything yesterday that may be of use to this case. Right, DS Irvine – we'll start with you. What did forensic tell us about the bridge?'

'They think that your suspicions are well-founded, sir,' revealed Irvine. 'The paint in the hub of the last knob had recently been rubbed. They agree that this was caused by a rope with a lot of tension rubbing against it. They found some rope hairs embedded in the paint.'

'Good start,' said Kennedy. 'I think we can assume that's how Berry came to be on that bank – he was lowered over the side of the bridge by someone using a rope. Good. Okay, who's next – let's keep this roll going,' Kennedy encouraged.

Yuppie-cop Lundy was next to report. 'We received good radio coverage yesterday evening on GLR. We're getting more this morning. We had twenty-six calls, all of which are currently being checked. The usual freaks – the most unusual from a member of an organisation he calls The Workers' League – they're threatening to kill one doctor a month until the government publicly announce an end to their destruction of the NHS. I'll keep you posted on anything that comes in that seems interesting, sir,' reported Lundy proudly.

'See that you do. And now, WPC Coles. Did you find out anything on your travels?'

'Not really, sir – but from what I can gather, William Jackson is a bit of a wimp and it would seem that Susanne Collins had, in fact, ended whatever kind of relationship they'd had. Apparently, Jackson kept pestering Susanne to continue with him.'

'Did his harassment turn physical at all?' inquired Kennedy.

'No, not at all, he was just being a drip, letting himself down in front of everyone and embarrassing her. It also seems that William Jackson is a pot-head.'

'Really?' laughed Kennedy. 'I haven't heard that term since the early seventies.'

'Yes, he's known to use hashish. Supposedly, he even smokes it in the staff common-room at school. Sometimes the headmaster comes in opening all the windows saying, "Weird smell in here, isn't there? I must have the janitor check the drains".' Coles laughed.

'So what did Trevor Davies have to say about William Jackson?' Kennedy asked Irvine, once the laughter had begun to subside.

'He claims he's really sick of looking after Jackson. He also admitted that Jackson used drugs and that it had a habit of making him unstable. It seems that when Susanne Collins died in hospital, Jackson's paranoia reached a peak that he went on a pill-binge for days. Trevor Davies doesn't like Jackson much. They met when they were both at college, and he feels that if he doesn't do something to help Jackson, no-one else will. I get the idea that Davies is worried that if Jackson does something stupid, he'll be partially to blame because he didn't help when he could.'

Several disbelieving eyebrows were raised around the room.

'Davies reckoned that Jackson survived by laying this guilt trip on everyone around him. He did the same with Susanne Collins. He tried to latch on to her in a moment when she showed pity for him. Jackson has an ever-increasing circle of people trying to get away from him.'

'Any more?' asked Kennedy.

'Yes, Davies says that Jackson hadn't in fact disappeared at the time of Berry's death but was blitzed out of his brains in his flat. Davies then spent some time with him, weaning him off the pills, though Jackson was still smoking pot. After a while, Davies thought that Jackson was back on the rails again, so he left him. But when

Jackson learnt that we'd been around the school asking questions, he freaked out again and was off on another binge. That was when you and I visited Jackson at his flat and came across Davies, sir.'

Kennedy nodded. 'And is that the lot?'

'Well, only that Davies also agreed that Susanne Collins really wanted to have nothing to do with Jackson. She just felt sorry for him. Jackson mistook this pity for something stronger and had high hopes of the two of them being together. But there never really was a scene going on between them.'

'Did Davies say whether or not Jackson was aggressive or violent at any time?' Kennedy quizzed.

'No, I don't think he did, sir, though he did describe Jackson as a weed.'

'Right, that leaves you, DC Milligan from Wimbledon. And what did your day turn up?'

'Nothing, sir.'

'Sorry?

'Er… nothing, sir. Sorry.'

'Nothing like getting to the point – an admirable quality, I know. But in this instance I had hoped for, shall we say, something,' Kennedy replied.

'Sorry, sir. I can tell you about their daily trip. Neither Junior nor Martin remember anything else about that morning. But I did check the one thing I thought was weird,' Milligan continued, gaining in confidence.

'And what was that?' asked Kennedy, liking this young DC more and more for his directness, intuitiveness and seeming lack of ego.

'It's just that I thought it strange that Martin had heard the splash and Junior hadn't, even though Junior was seemingly closer to the splash,' Milligan explained.

'And?' Kennedy prompted.

'Well, I stood by Junior's side and the roar of the engine would definitely drown out most noises. Martin, on the other hand, was in the main cabin with the windows open, so that's probably how he heard the splash – through the windows. The main cabin is somewhat insulated from the sound of the engine.'

'You're probably right. Anything else?'

'Just a small thing, more of an idea really,' Milligan offered, slightly nervous about voicing an original idea.

'It's okay,' Kennedy said in his soft voice. 'Most of my good ideas start their lives as silly ideas – hopefully, they develop into something.'

'Well, sir – I hung around the Cumberland Basin for a time. For the duration of one of the boat trips in fact. And I stood on the bridge – you know, at the point where you figured Berry was lowered from. And I was trying to imagine what might have happened.'

The team was intrigued.

'And I couldn't.'

The team smiled.

'Then I thought that someone must have come up with a very clever plan to work all this out. I figured that it must have been someone who knew the area quite well, someone local. But then I thought that, if it were me, I wouldn't do anything like that too close to home. I mean, er… sir, that, of course, I would never do anything like that in the first place, sir…'

'I'm sure you wouldn't.' Kennedy laughed.

'But if I did, I'd find somewhere that couldn't be connected to me. I thought about which people would know the place well enough to work out a plan but with no obvious connection. And then I saw it, sir – the Feng Shang Boat Restaurant. Our murderer could have dined in there and surveyed the scene without drawing attention to himself and worked out the whole plan. He'd have a great overview of the entire scene, sir. And I was thinking that, if it's okay, sir, we could check with the restaurant and go through a list of their credit-card diners for the last month or so to see if any of the names are familiar,' the DC concluded.

'Great, Detective Constable – good thinking,' approved Kennedy.

Milligan was blushing from the attention.

'But, of course, there has to be a chance that if our murderer did dine there – and I'm well prepared to accept that he did – perhaps he paid in cash. But it's worth a go. You get straight down there and go through those credit card receipts.'

Kennedy addressed the entire team. 'Good thinking, eh?' They nodded their agreement. 'That's one of the secrets of our trade: always try to put yourself in the murderer's shoes. Try to go through the options that would be open to him (or her) and somewhere in the middle of it all should be a solution. Now, let's look at this again and see what we can see. Okay?'

Chapter Thirty-one

The posse watched Kennedy rise from his desk and go over to the case noticeboard. 'Right – we have our victim, Dr Edmund Berry,' Kennedy said, pointing to the picture on the noticeboard. He continued. 'Now – so far, we have only two suspects, it would seem – Norman Collins and Michael Jackson.'

The room reverberated with laughter.

Kennedy took a moment to realise what he'd said. 'Sorry,I mean William Jackson. Michael has an alibi for that morning – he was with Bubbles his monkey and Bubbles will swear to that.'

More laughter. When they'd settled down, he continued. 'Let's start with Norman Collins – he certainly has a motive. Berry was attending his sister when she died. Collins is a passionate man and very strong. I spoke to him in Derby yesterday – that's right, I wasn't idle yesterday – and he told me that on the morning in question, he had caught the six o'clock train from Derby to London, arriving in London at seven-fifty – too late, it would seem, to arrange and carry out the murder. But if he caught the 3am train from Derby, that would put him into St Pancras at five-thirty-seven. He has a railway employee pass and would not have needed to purchase a tell-tale ticket. If he did catch the earlier train, then this certainly would have given Collins enough time to pick up Berry, take him to Cumberland Basin, and lower him down on to the bank.'

Irvine nodded in agreement.

'Now, maybe he was about to kill Berry when he was interrupted by Junior arriving, prior to setting off with the Sailing Diamond. So, he then had to hide in the shadows and the minute that the Sailing Diamond cast off, he dumped the drunken body of Dr Berry into the water. He would have hung around for a period of time to make sure that Berry did not arise from his watery grave. Collins would still have had time to attend to his pigeons and catch the nine o'clock train back home. He would have needed to, because he clocked into work at one o'clock.'

'Wouldn't he have let the pigeons off first, sir?' asked Coles.

'No, he couldn't. Pigeons won't fly in the dark which is why, in normal circumstances, he would not have caught the earlier train,' Kennedy answered, sharing some of his newly acquired pigeon knowledge.

Irvine spoke next. 'But how would he have moved around London, sir – a body and some pigeons would stick out a bit. By car perhaps? Taxis are out.'

'No and no: too noticeable and traceable. Let's check if Susanne Collins had a car and if she did, find out where it is now. Anyway, the Collins case is flawed, I know, and there are more than a few missing links, but we have to make a start somewhere.'

Kennedy took a quick breather, allowing the team an opportunity to mull over these new developments.

'Okay, we'll get on. Our other suspect is William Jackson – let's look at him. Are we to believe that he's a pot-head and a wimp, totally incapable of committing such an act? But what if this is no more than an image he's cultivated? What if Jackson, instead of being totally bombed or blitzed or whatever words are used to describe the current state of drug haze, was in fact, totally in command of his senses and well able to pick up Berry and go through the procedure I've just described?'

'He certainly has a motive, sir,' suggested Coles.

'Aha, I agree. He was losing the girl, though in fact, he'd already lost her, so he wouldn't have felt the pain to the same degree as Norman Collins. I'm not sure about this one either, but suspects are kind of thin on the ground at the minute, so we better hold on to all that we've got.'

'What about Dr Burgess?' asked Irvine.

'Burgess?' muttered Kennedy.

'Well, sir – Staff Nurse Butler told me that the word around the wards was that Burgess' wife is – or was – having a secret affair. Some of the gossip, and it may just be gossip, was that the affair was with Berry. Of course, it could just be a case of two beautiful people and the tongue-waggers putting two and two together and getting five. But suppose they were having an affair? Burgess treats his wife likes one of his prized possessions. He obviously doesn't want to lose her, so he might have topped Berry to save face and keep his wife.'

Kennedy was clearly interested in this latest line of thought, so he had Irvine elaborate.

'He'd have had a much better opportunity than either Jackson or Collins. He could have got in and out of the hospital easily and would have known Berry's whereabouts and movements far better than the other two.'

'Interesting, very interesting, but just not possible, Sergeant,' concluded Kennedy.

'Why's that, sir?' inquired Irvine, puzzled at Kennedy's certainty.

'Because at the precise time Berry was heard splashing into Regent's Canal, his colleague, Burgess, was on duty at the hospital and I imagine there are a few dozen witnesses who could confirm this. Now, if this was a crime novel, I'm sure they'd find some way to tie Burgess in with this crime. I'd certainly not be surprised to find out that he was a murderer, but unfortunately – though fortunately for him and other innocent suspects – that is not a possibility. No , I think we can rule Burgess out.'

There were no more voices of dissent so Kennedy issued his orders. 'Let's do this. Let's get our friends in Derby to ask around the railway station and find out if anyone actually remembers Norman Collins catching the three o'clock train – or even the six o'clock. Let's also try and find an alibi – or not – for William Jackson. I must admit, he's the one I'm most suspicious of. I don't know why I think that, I don't feel it in my bones, I don't feel it in my water, I don't see it in my tea-leaves, it's just a good healthy suspicion.'

Irvine cracked a smile.

'We'll also see what the public response is to our radio and press appeals and see if maybe we should cast our net a bit wider.' Kennedy turned to Coles . 'You and I will visit Sheila Berry again and see, now that she's had time to think about it, if she has any suspicions. And maybe we should also call on Mrs Burgess – what's her first name?' Kennedy thought for a few seconds and then answered his own question. 'Amelia, yes, that's it, Amelia Burgess. Let's see how she and her alleged boyfriend – whoever he is – fit into the picture.'

The meeting was over.

Kennedy had drunk four cups of tea during the course of the session and he was using a fifth to wash down the last of the doughnuts. Talking is thirsty work.

Chapter Thirty-two

As WPC Coles drove Kennedy up to England's Lane, she had the sense of him being more attractive than she remembered. Not that Kennedy was coming on to her or anything like that – it was simply that his sexual body-language seemed somehow more assured. The WPC wondered why she had failed to notice this before; she also wondered whether Kennedy had a girlfriend or not. Socially, he kept himself to himself and there was never any gossip around the station about his private life. To the outside world, Kennedy seemed to be a contented, enlightened man, totally committed to the art of criminal detection.

Kennedy, in his current clueless state, would have been very happy to know that the team were totally convinced that he would solve the crime. They were equally satisfied that he could solve each and every case put on his desk. He would be even further flattered if be knew that his team – or posse, as he called them – was the favourite team in the division. They all appreciated the way they were treated as equals and encouraged to help solve the cases. The more usual situation was for the soldiers to do the legwork and, upon completion of the case, the leader would take all the credit.

But at that precise moment, Kennedy could be doing with a bit of that faith and confidence himself. He had a victim, a victim whom Kennedy was convinced had been murdered, but there were still no clues to show how the murder had been committed. He had two suspects but time was passing fast and to Kennedy's way of thinking, that meant that the trail was growing colder.

Perhaps it was because of the wondrous blue sky overhead, but the doom and gloom seemed to have risen from the Berry household. Perhaps it was because Sheila Berry was trying really hard to make her son's life as comfortable and as normal as possible. As she greeted the WPC and Kennedy, she was bent almost double: one hand on the Yale lock opening the door and the other restraining Sam by the scruff of his neck.

'Oh, good morning – good to see you again. Come on in quickly, won't you. Every time Sam hears the doorbell ringing, he wants to go outside,' she explained.

'Good morning, Mrs Berry,' said Kennedy. 'We've come to ask you a few more questions, I'm afraid.'

'Why don't you go straight through to the kitchen – I'll make some tea. What about you, Sam, do you want some tea with the kind policeman and policewoman?'

'Cups,' spluttered Sam.

'Yes,' his mother agreed. 'You can get the cups.'

Kennedy relayed his new information to Sheila Berry. He told her how he had reached the conclusion that her husband had not committed suicide.

She seemed relieved to hear this – somehow, this news was consoling. Mrs Berry and her son could not live their lives with the obloquy of Dr Berry's death. Kennedy noticed that just as she seemed to be mentally shaking off one cloud, another descended on her – the realisation that her husband had been murdered.

'So, who do you think killed my husband and why?' she asked.

'Well, that's what I've come to talk to you about – to see if you can help us shed any light whatsoever on the case. Can you think of anybody who might have wanted your husband dead?'

Kennedy became aware of Sam's presence. 'Sam – would you like to play with Anne in the living-room while I talk with your mother?' Sam took Coles' hand and innocently followed her out of the kitchen, throwing a caring glance to his mother as he did so.

'I'm sorry, Mrs Berry,' continued Kennedy, his eyes fixed on the formidable woman before him, whose strength was returning bit by bit, day by day, 'but I have to try and find a motive for this. Is there anything at all you can tell me?'

She had been tempted to invite Kennedy to call her Sheila but had felt that it may be inappropriate and make him feel awkward. But she liked this man, she liked his warmth and compassion and it felt strange him addressing her as 'Mrs'.

'The only unpleasantness in our lives since we met, Inspector, was the death of that poor school teacher. But as I told you before, the only thing that Eddie said about that was it shouldn't have happened.'

'He said nothing more about it – you're sure?'

'No, just words to the effect of how it shouldn't have happened, and what should he do? I told him that there was nothing that he could do about it now. But he hadn't been listening, he just snapped out of it and we continued talking about something else. You think that it's connected in some way, don't you? The death of the school teacher?'

Kennedy nodded. 'I think it could be, yes.'

'But patients die unexpectedly all the time. I don't see why there should be a connection,' she ventured.

'Nevertheless, Mrs Berry, since we last spoke, have you thought of anything that might have troubled your husband: money, debts, bad blood, arguments at work, maybe something in his family, anything at all?'

'No. Nothing that I am aware of. Murder is a pretty drastic solution and I honestly cannot think of anything that would in any way add up for you.'

'What about… I'm sorry to ask you this again… but what about other women. Were there any?'

'I can only be honest with you,' she interrupted. 'We had a gloriously active sex life.' She blushed ever so slightly. 'I don't know how to say this without making it sound sordid, but after we had finished with each other there was nothing left for anyone else – nothing left at all.'

Now it was Kennedy's turn to blush slightly.

Sheila Berry was speaking more quietly now. 'I thought when we first met that the sex was wonderful but that once the novelty of the newness of each other's bodies had worn off, we would tire of each other and that it would slow down a bit. But the more we knew each other, the better it became – it was blissful. I couldn't believe how divine it was. We discussed how magical it was. In truth, we couldn't keep our hands off each other.'

Kennedy's blush deepened to scarlet. Here he was with this exquisite, graceful woman, and she was telling him her intimate secrets. For the second time she left him with no reason to disbelieve her.

'I'm sorry to put you through this,' he said quietly.

She was silent for a moment, perhaps reminiscing. 'No. It's good to talk about it. You know, I miss him a lot and I miss making love with him. At first, I felt guilty that I was missing our love life, but now I feel no guilt at all. Don't get me wrong – I don't miss sex. I don't long for or need sex. I just miss making love to him. Do you see the difference, Chris… Inspector?'

'Yes, yes I do,' Kennedy replied, and he thought of ann rea as Sheila Berry was thinking of Edmund Berry.

Chapter Thirty-three

The contrast between the two households was stark. The house Kennedy and Coles had just left was warm, lived-in; it smelled of family life and home-cooking and there were fresh flowers all over. It was a house that was busy but not untidy. Amelia Burgess' home on the other hand, was spotlessly clean and oddly clinical. It was more like a show-house than a home. The predominant smell was that of perfumed disinfectant. Not a speck of dust or any blemish in sight. Obviously, a palace suitable for Dr Burgess to entertain in.

As Kennedy entered the house, a slight twinge reminded him that (firstly) he had drunk about seven cups of tea so far today and (more importantly) he had not visited the toilet since his first cup.

Amelia Burgess was not as Kennedy had expected her to be. She looked as if she felt just as uncomfortable in the house as Kennedy and the WPC did. She showed them through to the study and left them as she went off to organise some coffee.

'Actually, tea for me, please,' Kennedy had said, before getting down to browsing around.

He glanced through Dr Burgess' rows and rows of books. There was the expected medical section alongside his desk. A large section of extremely expensive-looking and noticeably unread leather-bound classics was prominently displayed. Some of them were probably priceless first editions, Kennedy thought.

There was another large section of popular modern novels. Kennedy noticed several titles from the current best-seller list. He also noticed what looked liked a complete set of Jeffrey Archer novels. Smiling, Kennedy took down Archer's *Shall We Tell the President*, to see if it was a first edition. Indeed it was, and inscribed – *To Spencer Burgess. Thanks for your contributions and support. All the best, Jeffrey Archer.*

P.G. Wodehouse was here, too – Kennedy reckoned there must be nearly one hundred titles on the shelves. Underneath that section was a shelf reserved for manuals, reference books, cook-books – there was even one entirely devoted to potatoes. Kennedy was surprised at the number of edible things one could produce with potatoes these days.

Not surprisingly, Burgess also possessed books about books,

including *How to Buy Rare Books* by William Rees-Mogg. There were books on wine and, weirdest of all, a book about knots – the colourful, *Complete Guide to Knots* – clearly as an aide to Dr Burgess' nautical pastime.

Above the book-shelf was a large autographed oar. Kennedy was trying to make out the names when Mrs Burgess returned.

'Sorry, no tea. Hope coffee will do,' she announced as she strode through the door with a tray in her hands. She closed the door behind her with her foot and Coles and Kennedy joined her at the coffee table.

Kennedy was not really a coffee man, just now and again – actually, twice a year maximum, but he accepted it. 'Very, very milky with two sugars, please.'

Mrs Amelia Burgess had also supplied delightful paper-thin shortbread. Kennedy desperately wanted to dunk the shortbread in his coffee but he could see, over his hostess' shoulder, the image of his mother watching him and mouthing the words, No, you mustn't do that.

As the coffee passed his lips for the first time, he felt another twitch and moved his legs closer together.

'Well, Chief Inspector – what can I do to help you?' she asked.

'Detective Inspector, actually,' smiled Kennedy, before continuing. 'We're investigating the murder of a colleague of your husband – a Dr Berry.'

'Murder? Oh, yes, Spencer told me about that. He said that the police thought that it was murder but he felt it was either suicide or an accident,' she suggested before adding, 'So how can *I* possibly help you?'

'Did you know Dr Berry at all?'

'Vaguely. I met him several times at functions with my husband. I didn't know him very well but he seemed a nice enough fellow.'

'When was the last time you saw him, Mrs Burgess?' questioned the detective.

'Oh, let me see – several weeks back. Probably before Christmas. Yes, that would have been it, at one of the hospital's horrid Christmas parties.'

'So you were no more than an acquaintance and you hadn't seen him since December,' asked Kennedy, now crossing his legs to ease his discomfort.

'No, we were no more than acquaintances and I had not seen him since December,' she said indignantly before continuing, 'and what on earth do you mean by that?'

'Well, I don't really know how to put this but…' Kennedy really felt awkward, helped none by his need to visit the toilet.

'Yes?' she insisted.

'It has been suggested to me, Mrs Burgess, that you and Dr Berry were…' Kennedy uncrossed his legs again and pushed his knees very tightly together – 'Were… well, more than acquaintances.'

'What? What on earth… oh dear, Inspector, are you suggesting that…' She broke out laughing. 'Suggesting that we are – sorry – *were* lovers?'

'I don't see what's so funny about it, Mrs Burgess.'

Kennedy really did wish he had asked her for the use of the toilet when they arrived. He had fully intended to do so but the place was so posh he could imagine Dr Burgess coming home that night and on his first visit to the little-boys' room shouting out, 'Here Amelia, love – who's been dribbling on my seat?'

Amelia Burgess was still laughing and Coles looked over at Kennedy nervously. He seemed to be twitching an unusual amount as well.

'Well, I suppose I better tell you because you'll find out anyway with all your sniffing around. Yes, Inspector , I do have a lover, but it was not, I assure you, your poor Dr Berry. You see, my lover is a woman. I'm gay, lesbian, homosexual – whatever you want to call it, you quaint man. My lover and my husband are both well aware of each other's existence. My husband and I, we use each other. He wanted a pretty wife, another of his expensive possessions. He wanted me to be his caring, doting, darling wife and I wanted the lifestyle, the money and the freedom to be with my lover. So, Spencer and I…well, we worked out this arrangement.'

Kennedy wasn't sure how much longer he could hold on.

'There are lots of unwritten conditions but as long as I don't embarrass him publicly, he doesn't mind what I do. My lover and I don't mind my play-acting, we are genuinely in love but have never felt the need to be part of some exclusive club to prove it. So you see, Inspector – we each have what we want. But I'm sorry, Dr Berry did not fit into our cuddly threesome.'

She concluded just as Kennedy was about to burst.

He rose quickly and said, 'I'm sorry, Mrs Burgess. Please forgive me if I embarrassed you.'

'I assure you, Inspector,' she smiled, 'I'm not the one embarrassed.'

Chapter Thirty-four

On returning to his office, Kennedy had two telephone messages – one from Burgess, who wanted Kennedy to ring him back, and one from ann rea, who was 'out and about' and would call later.

Tea first, thought Kennedy, now a very happy man having made room (thanks to a quick toilet-stop at The Queens), for more tea. He brewed-up and managed to wolf down a couple of chocolate biscuits before settling down at his desk to phone Burgess.

'St Pancras All Saints Hospital.'

'Hello. Could I speak to Dr Burgess, please?' Kennedy requested.

'He's on another call at the moment, sir. Will you ring back or will you hold?' asked the hospital telephonist.

'Ah – I'll hold on for a while,' answered Kennedy.

He spent the few minutes tidying up his desk and staring at his case noticeboard hoping for inspiration.

'Dr Burgess is free now. Who shall I say is calling?'

'Detective Inspector Christy Kennedy of Camden CID,' Kennedy said quietly but confidently.

'Putting you through.'

There was a click and a high-pitched voice barked into Kennedy's ear. The noise was so unpleasant he couldn't make out any of the words that were being shouted at him. He held the earpiece away from his ear but kept the mouthpiece in its functional position.

After a while, Kennedy called out: 'Hello, if there's anyone there, I have to tell you that I can't make out a word that you may be saying, so if you would like to quieten down a few decibels perhaps we can talk. Until then, I'm not even trying to listen.'

The racket died down.

'Dr Burgess?' began Kennedy.

'Yes,' the doctor hissed.

'What's the prob...?'

'How dare you? How dare you go into my house? How dare you question my wife and how dare you – you excuse for a policeman – how effing dare you accuse her of having an affair with Berry? Hey?'

Burgess wasn't interested in Kennedy's reply and continued pouring his anger down the phone line. It oozed like chocolate sauce over ice-cream.

'How effing dare you? I'll be speaking to Superintendent Castle. I'll have you, you'll see. I'm not just one of your plebs, don't you know. You can't pull me off the street and beat an admission out of me. I've got connections – you'll see I'm connected. I can stop people like you trying to do this to people like me. Save that treatment for the poor people.'

Kennedy was nearly beginning to enjoy this.

'And if I ever – ever – hear the slightest whispers of the fact that my wife is… well, you know what she told you. How did you prise that information out of her, the poor woman? What did you threaten her with? Hey? I'm telling you, Kennedy, if I ever hear anything about my wife being, you-know, I will personally have you thrown off the police force and back into the gutter where you so obviously belong.'

There was more.

'It's all our business – nothing to do with you, nothing to do with Dr Berry. Open your eyes, man, can't you see that poor unfortunate man Berry botched up the diagnosis on that girl – that Collins girl – and if you had half a brain you would have realised that. But you're too busy trying to make a name for yourself, sticking your nose in other people's business. I don't have to pretend that I like you – I don't have to act scared of you. I don't need to be careful that I don't upset you in case you look at me closer or harass me. My wife has not done anything wrong. I have not done anything wrong. I do not have to put up with you nosing around in my business, so clear off and leave us alone.'

Kennedy could hear that the doctor was breathing heavily. He let a near-silence fall between them. After all that barking the silence was paradise.

'You there? Hello? Are you still there?' the doctor asked hoarsely.

Kennedy answered in a soft, calm voice: 'Have you finished now? Good. I'm afraid you lost me around the "I'm not a pleb" bit. But believe me, Doctor, I got the gist and I don't need it repeated. But now, I'd like you to listen to me for a couple of seconds. It's short and it's simple. I questioned your wife and as a result of that questioning I have ruled her out of my inquiries.'

Kennedy continued softly, so softly, in fact, that Burgess had to strain to hear the words.

'If you had half the class your wife has, you'd realise I do not need – or wish – to spread any information I may have learned while questioning your wife. If you wish to speak to Superintendent Castle, then I can let you have his telephone number. That's all I have to say.'

Kennedy heard some more shouting in the earpiece as he returned the handset to its cradle.

Ten seconds later the phone rang again. 'Yes!' Kennedy snapped.

'Kennedy?'

He was immediately remorseful. 'I'm sorry, ann rea. I've just gotten off the phone with that pompous prat, Burgess from St Pancras.'

'It's okay, I understand.' She was happy to see how quickly he had pulled out of his attitude once he had heard her voice. 'Look, I've been thinking. We've been friends for nearly a day now and you haven't asked me out to dinner yet.'

Kennedy took all of a split second to forget that the pompous prat Burgess ever existed.

'Yes, of course. Good. Let's have dinner.'

'You've such a way with words, Kennedy, you say the nicest things. I'll pick you up at six-thirty at North Bridge House, okay?'

'Perfect.'

'See you then, Kennedy.'

And she was gone. ann rea, the perfect tonic for pomposity.

Chapter Thirty-five

Kennedy stood outside North Bridge House in the cold evening air watching Parkway wind down. It had been another frustrating day and nothing had really fallen into place. The day before had been a day of progress, today a day of marking time, but in a murder enquiry you have to rely on both kinds of days in order to solve the crime.

ann rea pulled into the car park in her Ford Popular, a mean, clean machine she was proud of.

'Dinner at my place suit you, Kennedy?'

'Sounds great to me,' Kennedy replied, as he tried to figure out whether he should kiss her on the cheek or shake her hand. ann rea solved the problem by kissing the air a few millimetres from his face.

'It's a trick I've learnt at cocktail parties,' she said after they'd climbed into the car. She eased the car into gear and headed off towards her home in Hartland Road in nearby Chalk Farm.

'This is a bit nippy,' said Kennedy as car zipped through the traffic.

'Yes, it passes everything but a petrol station,' she laughed.

Pretty soon, it was parked outside ann rea's home.

'Come straight through to the kitchen. You can make some tea and I'll start dinner,' she announced, throwing her car and house keys on to a shelf on the hallway hat-stand.

Persuading Kennedy to make a cup of tea doesn't take a lot of work and soon he had filled the kettle and had the water boiling. ann rea systematically unpacked her Marks and Sparks shopping bags and stacked the contents into cupboards and fridge.

'What on earth did Burgess say to you to put you in such a foul mood earlier?' she asked.

'Ah, I just hate people like that and all they stand for. Where do you keep your tea?'

'Up there in the cupboard – directly above the toaster,' she pointed. 'But he must have really rattled your cage.'

She re-opened some of the cupboards and started to remove the ingredients for her dish of the night.

'Well, I went to chat to his wife to see if I could find out anything about Dr Berry,' he began, whilst heating the pot with a dash of water from the kettle to the point where it felt warm to his hands. He spooned in three teaspoons of leaf-tea, one for each person and one for the pot. When the water was boiled, he poured a dash into the teapot – not much, just half a cup-full or so – and swilled it around in the pot before adding the rest of the boiling water. Kennedy then set the teapot to one side and left the tea to brew. One of the many rules of tea-making he ascribes to is how important it is not to heat the pot at this point (as some people are wont to do), as this stews the tea. This is what happens in cafés and staff canteens in their endeavours to keep tea hot for long periods of time. Kennedy usually adds the milk to the cup before pouring the tea, followed by sugar, if required. Kennedy has two sugars, ann rea none.

'Kennedy, you do know how to make good tea,' said ann rea, taking her first sip. 'This is exactly what I need at this time of the day. I never thought I'd be able to say that about anything non-alcoholic.'

She continued to sip her tea contentedly.

ann rea leant back against the work-top on which she had set out the food. She held her left arm across her chest, cupping the elbow of her right arm in her left hand. In this manner, she supported the cup of tea in her right hand and, like a crane, swung the cup of tea to and from her mouth.

Kennedy was sitting at the dining-table, feeling guilty at the fact that his eyes – lacking subtlety – were obviously drawn to the weight now supported by her left arm. If she was aware of his eyes, her body-language did not admit it. She almost smiled at him, but not quite.

'So what did Mrs Burgess have to tell you about Dr Berry? What did she tell you that made her loving husband go so mad at you?' she asked, sipping her tea.

'Well, I asked her was there any truth in the rumours going around the hospital that she and Berry had been having an affair and…'

'Oh, you didn't, Kennedy?' she laughed in disbelief.

'Yes, I have to try and find some motive for the murder. Jealousy is an obvious one, though in this case, it probably wouldn't have done me a lot of good even if she had been having an affair with Berry.'

'Why, Kennedy?'

'Why? Because her darling, caring husband has the perfect alibi. He was on duty in the hospital at the time the murder was committed.'

'So how did Amelia react to your subtle line of questioning?'

'Well, she was amused, yes, amused more than anything else and she told me – you must keep this a secret, mind – that yes, she was having an affair but that it was with a woman. She has a long-time female lover and apparently Burgess is happy with the set up.'

'Why on earth did she tell you?'

'She said she thought I would find out anyway. She probably

didn't want me snooping around, kicking up dust. But you don't seem surprised, ann rea?'

'I already knew, Kennedy. Not everybody in the press has to print *all* the stories they have about people's private lives. She's not part of any gay movement or anything but she's seriously in love with an older woman and they've been together and happy for about ten years now.'

Kennedy felt like a fool.

'But enough of this gossip, Kennedy. Put some music on and open a bottle of wine – there's some in the fridge. And I'll start dinner,' ann rea said, rinsing her teacup in the sink.

ann rea had a very impressive tape and CD collection but Kennedy didn't hesitate in selecting *Rubber Soul*, another Beatles classic. He adjusted the volume for the opening chords of 'Drive My Car', before returning to the kitchen. He sat down and stared at ann rea.

'The wine, Kennedy, the wine. The tea is great, I know, but I could do with a little alcohol in my blood.'

'Ah, yes, sorry.' Kennedy plopped out the cork. 'Where do you keep the wine glasses or shall we use two straws?'

'Ho ho. The glasses are in the living-room.'

Returning with a pair of elegant wine glasses, Kennedy poured two generous helpings of wine.

'So, how is the Berry case going? Have you much work left to do on it?' ann rea asked, sipping her drink.

'Now, there's a thing. You see, you've just voiced a very popular misconception about the art of detection.'

'What?' she asked, surprised.

'You know, once you've spent a certain amount of time on a case, you can solve it. I'm afraid that only happens in *Inspector Morse*. You know for a fact that by the end of Colin Dexter's fine novels – or by the end of the TV show – Morse will have solved the case. The criminal will go to jail and Morse and Lewis will drive off in the red Jaguar in search of real ale. At least, they always do on the telly, drive off in a Jag, that is, it's a Lancia in the books. Whatever, case solved – roll the credits.'

ann rea, still busy preparing dinner, smiled at Kennedy's entertaining monologue.

'A real case is a bit like life and a bit like a computer: you know that all the facts and details are there somewhere waiting for you to find them, all you need to know is which keys you need to press. Once you start getting some details, the rest falls into place. Until then, you just have to plod on, hoping for a little luck.'

Kennedy refilled the glasses. 'This wine is great, you know.'

'Yes,' she smiled. 'So, Kennedy – back to the case. Who looks the most likely suspect to you?'

'Okay,' he said, rearranging the HP sauce bottle, the milk jug and the sugar bowl. 'Here are my three main suspects.'

He moved the props one by one to the centre of the table.

'Here,' said Kennedy, pointing to the milk jug, 'is subject number one. Mr Norman Collins. Motive? He thinks that through careless-ness, Berry killed his sister, Susanne Collins. Opportunity? Well, he was certainly in London on the morning of the death, but he claims he wasn't here until after the crime was committed. He could have caught an earlier train, which would have given him enough time to kill Berry and release his pigeons.'

Kennedy failed to register ann rea's puzzlement concerning the pigeons.

'Method? He would have had to call in at the hospital, find Berry, and somehow administer some soporific drug to him before he could transfer him by his own devices to Cumberland Basin. He would then have had to lower the comatose Berry over the side of the bridge by rope, climb down after him – again by rope – wait till the Sailing Diamond had left or was leaving, so that Martin and Junior wouldn't see him, before dumping the body in the water.'

ann rea continued with the preparation of the food. Kennedy noticed that she had arranged red and green peppers, spring onions, sweetcorn, washed but unpeeled potatoes and diced mixed vegeta-bles. He tried to work out what she was cooking. Failing to do so, he returned to the case.

'Norman Collins seems to be an honest man and you wouldn't imagine someone like him committing murder. But he may have been driven by the urge to see justice done. He loved his sister, and both he and his father felt a great loss at her death. This is not some-thing they've experienced before and perhaps Norman had a strong urge to seek revenge and vent his anger, anything to ease the pain.'

Next, the sugar bowl took centre stage.

'Suspect number two, Mr William Jackson. Motive? He feels that Berry killed the girl he imagined was his girlfriend or the girl he hoped would become his girlfriend. Method? Would have to be something very similar to that described for Norman Collins. However, I have to say that somehow he seems a less likely suspect. I see him more as a weak man lost in a world of pot. I very much doubt that he would have had the wherewithal to execute such a complicated sequence of events,' Kennedy mused. 'Plus, our murderer had to be strong to move the body around the way he did.'

ann rea put her culinary task temporarily on hold.

'How about this for a theory, Kennedy?'

'Yeah, go on.'

'How about our friend William Jackson?' Taking up her glass of wine, ann rea crossed the room to sit beside Kennedy. She put her hand around the sugar bowl and moved it a bit to the left. 'What if suspect number two realises that Susanne Collins was, in fact, never going to be his or with him. So he can't live with that, she was his last hope. He's getting further and further into drugs, and she's told him "no way, José". So he finds a way to inject her with something that makes her blood thicken – it starts to clot, she falls in the schoolyard, goes to hospital and dies. And our hero gets to overplay the grieving boyfriend bit.'

Kennedy couldn't help but be impressed with ann rea's warped reasoning and he encouraged her to continue.

'All right… part two. What if our Dr Berry, in his examination of Susanne Collins, finds out exactly what had happened and is going to go to the police with his information. You did say that he had an appointment with his solicitor, perhaps that was going to be the topic of conversation. "How do I approach the police with this and not get myself into trouble?" Still with me, Kennedy? Good. Now, somehow, William Jackson finds out that Berry is about to spill the beans and so he murders his second victim. Jackson does this to cover up the fact that his first victim, Susanne Collins, was just that, a murder victim and not a freak death.'

'Hmm. Yes… okay. I know this William Jackson is not a very nice character and as a failed member of the human race, he's a more likely suspect than Norman Collins. It's just that I can't see Jackson being able to carry out the murder. I can't see him being able to lower Berry's body over the bridge and then climb down the rope himself. Then the real hard bit, climb back up the rope. Pulling up his own weight, not a task for a weakling. It takes a very fit man to climb up a rope.' Kennedy sounded convinced but ann rea had definitely set his mind off on a tangent. Her theory made a lot of sense and would tie up a few loose ends.

ann rea returned to her cooking but was into the swing of her story. 'Okay, Kennedy – you say our friend Jackson is a pot-head and a pill-popper. Well, we all know that the drug people are in each other's pockets. It wouldn't have been hard for him to recruit one or two of his mates to help him out.'

Kennedy mulled it over. 'So you think both deaths are connected? Interesting. The connection has to be Susanne Collins. The other thing they have in common, I suppose, is that both deaths have been made to look like something else. Collins, a hospital accident and Berry a suicide. I don't know, I'm still not sure.'

John Lennon interrupted Kennedy's train of thought, claiming he'd rather 'see you dead little girl than to be with another man' – 'Run for Your Life' – the last track on *Rubber Soul*. Kennedy thought this uncanny; was it a coincidence or a clue from on high? He drew ann rea's attention to this tip from the beyond. She smiled, saying that, as ever, The Beatles were in tune.

Kennedy doubted if he could convince his Superintendent that Lennon and McCartney's lyrics could be used as evidence to convict William Jackson. 'Well, you see, sir – it's like this. The Beatles sang me the answer to the case.' Yes? He didn't think so.

Kennedy returned to the living-room to select some more music. This time he opted for *Revolver*.

'I didn't know you were a Beatles nut,' called out ann rea.

Kennedy re-appeared in the kitchen. 'Well, they are the best,' he asserted, 'and that's the simple truth.'

They tuned into The Beatles for a couple of songs, ann rea continuing with her cooking and Kennedy mulling over the possibility of William Jackson being responsible for the death of both Susanne Collins and Dr Berry.

Towards the end of 'Eleanor Rigby', Kennedy wandered over to ann rea. 'What exactly are you making?' he asked, topping up the wine glasses. 'I feel very guilty sitting over there drinking your wine while you do all the work.'

'Don't worry about it, Kennedy, you're doing the dishes.' She laughed, her eyes buckling Kennedy's knees. 'It's nothing fancy. I call it "Psychedelic Potatoes".'

'No drugs in it, I hope!'

She laughed her brilliant laugh. Her eyes lit up the room when she laughed, he thought she looked so radiant. Kennedy was sure his heart was beating faster and he felt short of breath. Either he was having a mild heart attack or else he was falling in love with this incredible woman.

'No, Kennedy; no drugs. I hide them when you come around,' she laughed. 'Just potatoes – mashed in their skins – and some butter. Add sweetcorn, diced mixed vegetables courtesy of Bird's Eye, red peppers, green peppers and diced spring onions. Mix it all up and we have "Potato Psychedelia'", which is now ready, so set the table.'

Pretty soon, the two of them were tucking into the food.

'So what about the HP sauce?' asked ann rea.

'What?'

'The HP sauce?'

'It's there.' Kennedy pointed to the bottle.

'I know it's there, you fool,' she grandstanded. 'I mean, what about suspect number three?'

'Ah,' he smiled. 'My third suspect has a perfect alibi and no motive that I'm aware of – but perfectly positioned for the execution of the crime.'

'Dr Burgess?' she inquired.

'The very same!' he replied.

Chapter Thirty-six

The wine haze blurred Kennedy's remembrance of the previous night's events, but the friendliness of the evening shone through brightly. He and ann rea had continued their discussion over dinner, which had surprised him that something so simple could taste so incredibly delicious.

Kennedy had managed to keep The Beatles top of the night's play-list with five of their albums making it into the CD player before ann rea's protests had produced one of her favourite albums, *A Walk Across the Rooftops* by The Blue Nile. Kennedy had never heard it before but – maybe due to the combination of good wine and good company – the music had left an indelible mark on his memory and he now regarded it as one of the best albums he had heard in ages. As he browsed through his inter-office memos, Kennedy made a mental note to purchase a copy of the CD at the next opportunity.

Kennedy had hoped that the night might have ended with more than the peck on the cheek he had received from ann rea as she escorted him to his minicab. But, he now mused, if it's going to happen, it must happen naturally. Pleasant though the thoughts of the previous evening were, it was time to return to the case in hand.

Recalling ann rea's double-murder theory, he concluded that it was too far-fetched to be a real possibility.

There was a knock on his door.

'Come in.'

Detective Constable Milligan entered.

'So, Milligan, what have you for me this morning to get the day off to a fine start?'

'Sir, it's about the boat restaurant,' he began.

'Yes?'

'Well, I visited it and asked them if I could see the credit card slips for the period mid-January to early February. I was then left in a room to examine them.'

Kennedy was convinced that the young DC was getting somewhere, although he was not entirely sure where. But he decided to let him continue at his own speed.

'Well, I'm sorry to have to report, sir, but there was only one name on the slips that I recognised.'

'And whose was that?' asked Kennedy.

'Dr Burgess. No good is it, sir? Doesn't he have a solid alibi?'

'Just when did he eat there?'

Detective Constable Milligan consulted his notes. 'Friday 29th January, sir. He ate alone. The bill came to eighteen pounds and fifty pence and he left a two-pound tip making twenty pounds and fifty pence altogether.'

'Hmm, good work. Good work. Do me a favour will you? Dig up a photograph of our Dr Burgess and go back to the boat restaurant and see if any of the staff recognise him from his photo. Try and find out exactly where he sat, just to see if it fits in with your theory about the doctor over-viewing the Basin from his seat.'

'Erm, bit of a long shot, isn't it, sir?'

'Possibly, but that's what detective work is all about. Anyway, well done so far.'

Kennedy showed the proud young Milligan to the door.

'And while you're pushing your luck, see if they can remember anything about him – how he was dressed, was he relaxed or anxious? Anything you can dig up. Well done – very good work.'

'Funny people, these guv'nors,' Milligan said to Coles a few minutes later out in the corridor. 'You tell them something which can be of no use to them and they congratulate you on doing a good job. Funny people.'

'They're not the only ones,' smiled Coles as she watched Milligan walk down the corridor, shaking his head.

Chapter Thirty-seven

'Well,' said Kennedy to Irvine – 'I think it's time to go and see our favourite staff nurse again.'

'Count me in for that, sir,' Irvine eagerly chipped in. 'I'll drive.'

'Good idea, Sergeant. That way, we'll get there.'

Euston Road was busier than usual and they were stuck in traffic for a period equivalent to the lifetime of many species of insect. The rain was falling fast and steady, as it had done since dawn, producing a bleak, grey, miserable morning.

Kennedy tuned the radio into GLR to see what was happening in the world. The presenter was interviewing Colin Dexter about his new Inspector Morse novel.

'That's who we need to sort this out for us,' Kennedy proclaimed.

'Who sir?'

'Colin Dexter. Yes, we need Colin Dexter's brain to sort this one out. I wonder what it would really be like, though, if you brought Dexter or one of these other crime writers into a real case, have them attempt to solve a real-life crime,' Kennedy said, continuing his own thread. 'Apparently, the force did try it with Sir Arthur Conan Doyle way back when.'

'How did he get on?' inquired Irvine.

'I can't remember. His suspect turned out to be the murderer but the police didn't put the case together until six months later. Either that, or he was totally wrong, I must check up on it sometime.'

'I suppose it had to be one or the other,' Irvine said very quietly.

Kennedy turned the mild-mannered and amusing Dexter off with a flick of the switch as they drove into the hospital car-park.

'What exactly are we meant to be looking for this time?' inquired the detective sergeant.

'Well, I want to collect the duty rosters and I want to see if it would be possible for Burgess to "disappear" long enough to murder our Dr Berry.'

'Impossible,' Rose Butler answered when Kennedy asked her the same question a few moments later. 'No, he was actually on duty the entire time. If he had been on call, like Dr Berry had been a short time before, then he could have perhaps risked skipping off for a couple of hours, hoping that an emergency would not come in and require his presence. But Dr Burgess was on duty non-stop that morning.'

'Ah,' was all Kennedy could say.

'Let me fetch you copies of those duty rosters,' said the staff nurse, rising from her chair and giving Irvine a particularly warm smile as she left the room.

When she returned, Kennedy took the paperwork from her. 'Thanks. That's very helpful of you. One final thing, Staff Nurse.'

'Yes, Inspector?'

'Say I wanted to make someone appear to be drunk but I didn't want the bruise marks of a struggle from forcing a bottle of whisky down his throat. Is it possible? Is there any drug that you know of that would have the desired effect but would not show up in an autopsy?'

'Simple, Inspector, very simple. You'd just have to inject alcohol, whisky or whatever, directly into the bloodstream. That way would be a lot more effective than pouring a bottle of whisky down someone's throat as it's going straight into the bloodstream. It would also take effect near enough immediately.'

'Would it not take a long time, though, to inject the alcohol into the body?' Kennedy inquired.

She smiled. 'No. It's not like drinking eight shorts to become drunk – only a small percentage of those eight shorts would end up in the bloodstream. We're not talking about injecting half a bottle of whisky into a body using a needle, just a few millilitres.'

The nurse laughed.

Irvine laughed.

Then Kennedy laughed.

'Interesting,' Kennedy said, turning to Irvine. 'All right, Sergeant, I'm going to talk to Dr Taylor. Erm... maybe you could continue questioning the staff nurse and... er... see if you can find out anything else of interest.'

Kennedy left them giggling, and wandered along the corridor, up a flight of stairs, back along another long and bending corridor until he stopped at the door of Taylor's office.

'Good day, Inspector, fancy a cup of tea?' Taylor greeted him with a smile.

'Perfect. That's exactly what I fancy, old chap.'

'Good. Come in and sit down, I was just about to make myself one.'

The doctor made his way over to the sink area. He plugged in his electric kettle and washed out a couple of cups. His office was packed to overflowing with files and clips of paper and he had to turn sideways to negotiate his way past piles of papers to get to the sink area.

Kennedy had seldom seen such a crowded office but legend had it that Taylor could, within a couple of minutes, put his hand on any file required.

Carefully manoeuvring his way back to his desk – without spilling a drop of the precious tea – he handed one of the cups to Kennedy. Taylor's tea very much reflected the maker, not spectacular in the presentation but it delivered what was needed.

Kennedy savoured the first couple of mouthfuls of the piping hot tea before Taylor spoke. 'Well, Inspector, I know you love a cup of tea but I'm sure that's not the only reason you're here.'

'You're right.' Kennedy started off rather slowly. 'I want to discuss the Berry case.'

'Of course.' The doctor swivelled his chair around, cup of tea in one hand, and without spilling a drop, reached up on to a shelf behind him and produced a file marked *Berry, E.*

Kennedy marvelled at watching the legend at work before his very eyes; the magic filing system really did work.

Kennedy's smile remained on his face as he inquired, 'Would your examination notes tell you if Dr Berry had received any kind of hypodermic injection in the hours before his death?'

'Not really, no. But I'm intrigued; tell me more.'

Kennedy relayed the information he had just received about being able to inject a body with alcohol. 'Now, everyone tells me that Dr Berry drank only a little, if at all – but when his body was found, he was considered to have been "very drunk" prior to death. If this alcoholic state had been induced by someone pouring a bottle of whisky down his throat then some kind of struggle marks would have shown up in your examination.'

Taylor nodded his agreement.

Kennedy continued. 'Dr Berry was asleep, on call, so it would have been possible for someone to sneak up, inject him while he slept and then – while he was in this soporific state – he could have been carted off to the canal. The murderer was trying to make it look like either a drunken accident or a suicide. Do you think this theory will fly, Doctor?'

'Well, far-fetched as it is, it certainly has wings. Unfortunately I found no obvious injection marks. But, as all drug-users soon learn, there are plenty of places to inject the body that cannot be easily be detected,' concluded Taylor.

'Okay, Doctor. I understand. One other problem – if we accept that this is how Berry met his end, how could the murderer have taken his body out of the hospital without being noticed?'

Taylor thought for some time, during which they both sipped at their teas, taking warmth from the cups.

'Well, now – let me see. I suppose the most obvious way out of a hospital would be the easiest way into a hospital.'

'And what would that be?'

'In a wheelchair. One could cover the victim to make it look like a patient. And if the murderer puts on a doctor's white coat, he could walk around the corridors all night without anyone paying much attention.'

'Of course, of course!' exclaimed Kennedy. 'You're one hundred percent right. Great stuff!'

Kennedy was up and out of Taylor's office in a few seconds, shouting a hasty, 'And thanks for the tea,' behind him. He returned to Rose Butler's office in time to hear her saying to Irvine, 'You can tell that men are becoming the weaker sex, they're beginning to stand up and ask for their rights.'

Irvine blushed when he spied Kennedy.

'He's not asking you to make his tea already, is he, Rose? He's only known you a few days,' Kennedy joked. 'We've got to be off for now, but I should imagine one of us will be back to see you in the near future,' said Kennedy, winking at the smiling staff nurse.

Chapter Thirty-eight

J ust as they were about to pull out of the car-park, Kennedy asked Irvine to stop for a few seconds. He climbed out and crossed to where the car-park attendant was holed up. Irvine could see Kennedy ask the attendant a question. The attendant, in answer, pointed across the car-park to a large, black Range Rover. Kennedy nodded and returned to his own car.

'What was that all about, sir?' inquired the detective sergeant.

'Oh – I was just finding out what kind of car Burgess drives,' answered Kennedy.

They didn't talk much on the return trip to North Bridge House. Kennedy was thinking about his case, fitting the new pieces into an ever-growing and ever-changing jigsaw puzzle. Irvine, on the other hand, was considering the date he had just arranged for Saturday night with Rose Butler. Kennedy and Irvine were in the same car, on the same journey, but were a million miles apart.

'See you later,' called out Kennedy, as he eventually exited the car outside the front door of North Bridge House.

'Later, sir,' answered Irvine.

Kennedy, hands deep in pockets and still struggling with his mental jigsaw puzzles, strode straight to his office. He removed his overcoat, revealing a green waistcoat, white shirt, green tie and brown slacks, and his eyes homed in on the case noticeboard.

He scribbled more notes on sheets of paper and rearranged the noticeboard, hoping for inspiration. He felt he was making some kind of progress, but still couldn't feel that he had taken the major step he needed to feel comfortable with his progress.

He pushed the pin into the final sheet of paper and stood back, reviewing his arrangement of the Cumberland Basin case. Added to his earlier notes concerning Dr Berry, Norman Collins and William Jackson, was a new name: *Dr Spencer Burgess*. Below this was another sheet of paper on which Kennedy had written the following: *Wheelchair. Injection. On duty – alibi? Motive? Visits scene-of-crime.*

His phone rang.

'Hello?'

'Kennedy, what do you do at weekends?'

'Come again?' he replied.

'What do you do on weekends? Simple question.'

The query was vintage ann rea.

'Well, if I'm not in here, or out on a case, I stay at home and watch a video of the week's *Coronation Street*.'

'Pardon? Come on – I don't believe you. *Coronation Street*? Kennedy, please!'

'Why? What's wrong with that? Don't you like *Coronation Street*? I've been watching it for years, since it began, actually. I missed a few years and maybe I didn't see *every* episode, *every* week but enough to keep up with the plot,' he said proudly.

'Colour me impressed, Kennedy, you're full of surprises. I'm not sure I was expecting that to be one of them, though. You've totally thrown me... I've completely forgotten what I rang you about,' she laughed. 'Oh yes, that's it, the weekend. So what were you going to do this weekend?'

Kennedy was bemused. 'Well... actually, I was going to have a quiet weekend going over some of the notes and statements on the case, just to see if I've missed anything.'

'Okay,' she answered. 'Sounds good to me. How do you fancy doing that in Cromer? I have to do a "Winter Weekend in Seaside Resorts" article and I'm planning a leisurely drive up there tomorrow. I plan a pleasant Saturday evening, fit in a few interviews on Sunday morning and stop off for a nice riverside English Sunday lunch on the way back. So you could do your case research and revision while I'm doing my interviews.'

Kennedy was not as enthusiastic as one would imagine after such an invitation. 'Yeah, it sounds great,' he answered, sounding surprised and hesitant. His mind was running through the rooming arrangements and other such possibilities. His vocal hesitation was more from not believing his luck than from lack of interest for the trip. 'Did you draw the short straw?' he laughed, stalling a little.

'Kennedy – it's a great idea for an article. Lots of these places are ghost towns in winter. Boys off in search of female tourists who spent their summers there. Girls left behind like war brides now trying to conceal the fruits of their fortnight of passion with the visiting Romeos. The deserted seafronts – I can see Alan Whicker walking across the sands, microphone in hand – "Down here on the wind-swept coast which resembles the shape of a dog's hind leg, the local princess of candy floss sits on the frozen, lonely railings, weeping at the memory of her dreams shattered, like the ebbing tide now beating on the rocks beneath her, singing out –

He's gone, he's gone for good
You said that you would
If you only could.
He said you should.
You did, and now

He's gone, he's gone for good.'

Kennedy was in stitches. He'd never heard ann rea in such a funny mood.

'Ah, come on, Kennedy. It'll be fun!' she enthused.

'How can I resist? Cromer, it sounds great,' laughed Kennedy.

'Good. I'll book the rooms then, shall I?'

Ah, the horrible word 'rooms', thought Kennedy, although he wasn't sure why he thought or felt the rooms would have been anything but singular.

'Yes… great… yes, fine,' he stuttered.

'Okay, let's get an early start. I'll pick you up at, say, ten-ish, and we'll get there in time for lunch-ish. Great, Kennedy, see you then.'

'Erm… ann rea?' Kennedy began, but he was talking to telephonic white noise again – ann rea had disconnected.

A weekend away with ann rea, thought Kennedy. Such a possibility, a few weeks ago, would have been beyond his wildest dreams. Now that it was going to happen, he wasn't sure that it would necessarily fulfil his wildest dreams.

They seemed to be growing closer – but he was still not really sure where he stood. Was he doomed to be 'just a good friend' or was something more going to happen?

Such thoughts filled Kennedy's head as he packed up all the relevant files. He would brief Castle on the Cumberland Basin case before calling it a day – or even a week – now that it was Friday.

Time to go home and prepare for what would definitely not be a predictable two days.

Ready, steady… go! The weekend starts here.

Chapter Thirty-nine

'Kennedy! Kindly take your eyeballs out of your Alpen and replace them from whence they came. And while you're about it, close this,' said ann rea, gently putting her finger under his chin and pushing it delicately upwards. 'You're likely to catch flies.'

ann rea had walked into the breakfast-room on Sunday morning wearing something that was too light to be a pair of slacks but too heavy to be a pair of tights. Whatever they were, they hugged her picture-perfect figure like a second skin. The top, an emerald green affair, was stretched to bursting.

The shock for Kennedy was total. This was probably because he had not allowed himself – or, at least, not too often – to think of ann rea in this way. But here she was, leaving nothing to the imagination, large as life and twice as pretty.

Up to now, the clothes that she had worn in his company had never flattered her wondrous figure. That had probably been intentional but this, now, was sheer bliss: the much clichéd poetry in motion.

'God, Kennedy – stop staring!' she said, starting to turn crimson. 'Here, take a drink of your orange juice. It'll cool you down.' She passed him the glass. 'There, that's better, isn't it?'

'I'm sorry,' he whispered. 'It's just I wasn't expecting to see you… to see you dressed like this. I…' Kennedy uttered, shamefaced but gradually regaining his composure.

'Oh, it's okay, Kennedy. It's quite flattering really. I suppose part of me is… is pleased. But you'd better not get up from the table for a while,' she smiled.

Now it was Kennedy's turn to blush. But he was also quite pleased to be able to share this intimacy with ann rea. She was unveiling a familiarity that had been absent from their friendship before now.

'I've got it now,' he chuckled, totally recovering his composure, 'You're not really down here to do your "Alan Whicker Wintertime in British Seaside Resorts" article.'

'Oh?' ann rea inquired.

'Not at all. You're part of a plot to rid seaside resorts of male geriatrics. You go about each weekend to a different resort and when they see you looking like that, the old ticker can't cope and they drop like flies,' Kennedy joked.

'Oh, come on, Kennedy – it's Sunday,' she said coyly but enjoying their chat. 'Besides, I'd say that from the look on your face a few minutes ago, it's your ticker you should be worrying about.'

The weekend had certainly livened up.

They had driven across on Saturday, checked into their rooms in the Sandcliff Private Hotel and met for dinner in the hotel restaurant. After dinner, they went out in the cold night air to walk off their food. Kennedy suggested they stop off at a bar for a drink on the way back but, as the wine tasted second-hand, they returned to the hotel lounge and ordered tea. At about midnight – after a very pleasant conversation and a kiss on the cheek – they retired to their separate rooms.

Kennedy was unable to sleep for about an hour or so. He couldn't help but think about ann rea in her bed a few rooms away. He wondered if she was lying awake wondering about him lying awake wondering about her wondering about him. What would happen – or not happen – should he visit her room? Would such a visit put an end to their budding friendship? He reflected at the breakfast table that if he'd seen her last night in all her *ahem*, morning glory, then he was sure he wouldn't have had a wink of sleep all night.

'Okay, Kennedy, I'm going off with my trusty old recording Walkman to see who I can find to talk to and I promise that, in order to protect the older members of the parish, I'll wear a sensible over-coat. I'll pick you up at one-thirty, so be a good boy and get some work done,' ann rea ordered as she exited the breakfast-room after kissing him on the forehead and saying for the gawking company in her best Italian accent, 'Fanks fora mosta vondervul evenings darlings.'

Kennedy reddened again but his eyes remained glued to the graceful disappearing figure of ann rea – a vision as sweet as a good strawberry milkshake. He speculated on how long it would be before he saw her dressed this way again – if, indeed, he ever would. At the other end of the restaurant, his attention was diverted to a poor man who was receiving a proper ear-bashing from his partner for doing exactly what Kennedy had been guilty of.

Ten minutes later, he was back in his room. His attention now focused on the numerous files before him. He turned on the radio. There was no Capital Gold this far from London but he found a local station and it seemed to be in the middle of a country music show. Kennedy settled for that, took out his notebook and pen and started on the files.

Chapter Forty

Kennedy read on and on and on. After an hour or so, he emerged from his files and crossed the room to turn off the radio. He'd been quite enjoying the music. Perhaps that had been the problem: he feared he was enjoying the music so much he was distracted from the problem in hand. He didn't want to miss a vital clue or hint just because The Mavericks were getting to know the Knoxville Girl.

How brilliant that would be – to return to London with the case solved. Then maybe Kennedy could persuade Superintendent Castle that he should have similar weekends, at the department's expense of course, to solve other cases. If only…

The radio off, Kennedy put on the kettle to brew himself a cup of tea. Every hotel room these days seemed to be equipped with the 'in-room complete tea and coffee preparation kit'. As per usual, the preparation kit was supplied with long-life creamer, which was ghastly in tea. He sat down again at his notes, giving up on the liquid refreshment.

It was pointless; a couple of pages later and the total distraction of tea had again captured his attention.

He decided to walk down to order a jug of milk from the hotel reception, but found that his request met with typical intransigence.

'Now, sir – is that a cup of tea or a cup of coffee you'll be wanting with your milk?' inquired the receptionist.

'No, neither, actually. I just want a small jug of fresh milk,' Kennedy patiently explained.

'I'm sorry, sir, you can't have milk just by itself. Now, let's see what I can do for you,' she said, checking the room service sheet. 'How about some tea and toast, you'd be sure to get milk with that.'

'No thanks.'

She tried again. 'How about our keep-fit breakfast, sir? Now, that's great – freshly squeezed orange juice, muesli, wholemeal toast and tea with semi-skimmed milk.'

'No. Actually, I'd like just a jug of milk. A small jug of milk will do nicely, thank you.' Kennedy's fingers started to flex. 'You see, I'm just trying to make myself a cup of tea in my room.'

'Oh, that's easy, sir. I think you'll find that you have some milk there under your very nose in our 'in-room complete tea and coffee preparation kit'.

'That's not milk – that's cream. I don't like cream in my coffee – I like milk,' Kennedy said, testily.

'But, sir – just a moment ago you said you wanted a cup of tea. Now you're saying you don't take cream in your coffee. I'm afraid I'm getting rather confused.'

'I meant tea, of course – and I don't take cream in my tea. I rarely take coffee but, when I do, that's with milk as well. I don't like cream and I don't like long-life milk…'

'Well, sir – I'm sure if you tried it, you'd find that the long-life cream is not all that bad.'

'Oh, don't bother about it,' Kennedy answered sharply.

People were now staring and he didn't want to get into this. He had been having a pleasant morning and he was determined to continue to do so. He strode off and out of the door of the hotel.

The Sandcliff Private Hotel overlooked the seafront and Kennedy set off in the direction of civilisation. He silently wished ann rea good luck in finding people for her interviews as the streets were totally deserted. The only other time he could remember streets being as empty as this was when England played in the World Cup final, back in 1966. He imagined the 1990s equivalent would be the streets of Dublin, when Jack Charlton's Irish heroes were playing.

A couple of streets later – past signs for the putting green and penny arcade – Kennedy found a newsagents. He entered the shop – called simply, Devane's Shop – and found, to his delight, that they sold fresh milk. He crossed the empty shop to the fridge and took out a carton of milk. 'Success,' he said.

Kennedy put his hand in his pocket to pull out some change as he re-crossed the shop floor. His pocket was empty – he had left his hotel room without collecting any money from the table. He always emptied out his pockets on a desk or table, wherever he was – hotel, home or office.

He swore under his breath, returned the milk to the freezer and left the shop saying, 'Sorry,' to the assistant. This, he thought, was fast turning into a Ray Cooney farce.

'Enough is enough,' he said out loud as he returned to the hotel.

He could imagine the hotel reception staff whispering, Fussy bugger! as he passed them.

On entering the second-floor corridor, he spied a man leaving his room. 'Hello – can I help you? That's my room,' Kennedy announced from a distance.

The man was startled and spun around to face Kennedy. They eyed each other for a couple of moments.

'Erm… yes – I'm ever so sorry, sir,' the man began. He spoke with a soft lilt. 'I couldn't help overhearing your problem in the lobby, sir. You see, if they give you just a jug of milk, they can't charge you for

it, so they need to put something with it from the room service menu.
Then they can charge.'

'Ah, I see. Pity they didn't just explain all that,' answered
Kennedy.

He was closer now and could see the man was wearing a hotel
name tag – Francis Healy – a name worthy of the accent.

'So I slipped into the kitchen and borrowed a jug of milk for you.
When I arrived up here, there was no-one in your room, so I just left
the milk. I let myself in with a pass key.'

Kennedy smiled, half to himself and half to Francis Healy:
'Thanks. Thanks a million.'

'Grand so – enjoy your stay,' replied the hotel porter.

'Here, hold on a minute, let me get you something,' Kennedy said
as he slipped into his room. He checked everything was as he had left
it and collected a couple of pound coins. Kennedy would have
preferred a pound note – it always looked like more to him. 'There
you go, Francis, thanks a million.'

'Thank you, sir,' Francis said as he pocketed the money.
'Anything else you want, just give me a shout.'

They parted to continue with their respective days.

Kennedy made himself the long-desired (and now richly
deserved) cup of tea. He then contentedly returned to his files.

Ninety minutes and three cups of tea later, he spotted something
that made him sit up.

'A-ha!' he exclaimed.

He had been looking through the answers to the appeal on the
radio and in the newspapers and one response caught his attention.
The switchboard had received a telephone call from a Mr Peter
Dyson. It seems that early on the morning in question – Tuesday 2nd
February – Mr Dyson had spied a person pushing a wheelchair near
Cumberland Basin. The duty-officer obviously didn't feel this was of
earth-shattering importance so no further questions had been asked.

Dyson's telephone number, thankfully, had been recorded and it
was this very number that Kennedy now dialled.

'Hello,' the voice answered.

'Good morning, this is Detective Inspector Christy Kennedy. I'm
sorry to disturb you on a Sunday,' Kennedy said as he announced
himself.

'Oh, that's okay. I suppose you're ringing about this Cumberland
Basin affair.'

'Yes, Mr Dyson – that's correct. The report of your call caught my
attention. Would you remember what time you spotted this person
with the wheelchair?' Kennedy inquired.

'Yes, about 4.10 or 4.15am.'

'That's kind of early to be out and about isn't it?'

'Not for me, I work at the zoo across the road from Cumberland Basin. I was due to go on duty at four-thirty that morning and I always like to get in a little early. You know what it's like that time of the day, I like to lose the cobwebs from the brain before starting work. Anyway, I saw this guy – well, I didn't actually see a face so I suppose it could have been a woman – anyway, man or woman, I saw someone pushing a person in a wheelchair. Again, regarding the person in the wheelchair, I couldn't say whether it was a man or woman. As I was turning into the zoo, near the Broad Walk staff entrance, I saw this person and the wheelchair leaving the Outer Circle and heading over the canal on St Mark's Bridge. That's all I can remember. Sorry I can't be more helpful.'

'No, really, thanks. You've been helpful, very helpful. Would you mind just thinking back once more – did you see anything else that might be of interest?'

'Well, no, not that I can remember.' Dyson was quiet for a few seconds. 'No, just the wheelchair.'

'You didn't see where they came from?'

'No. They were crossing the bridge by the time I spotted them.' Kennedy thought about what else he could ask.

'Okay. What about vehicles, transport. Was there…'

'Of course – the Range Rover,' Dyson interjected.

'Range Rover?' Kennedy repeated.

'Yes, yes of course, I can see it now. There was a Range Rover parked on the Outer Circle, one wheel was up on the pavement.'

'Do you… would you remember the colour of the Range Rover, Mr Dyson?'

'It was black, Inspector, a shining, black Range Rover.'

'Great, great. You've been very helpful and, once again, sorry for disturbing your Sunday.'

'No, it's perfectly all right, Inspector. I'm glad I could help. It's good to know that the police are working right through the weekend; makes you feel more secure.'

Kennedy felt just a tiny bit guilty.

Chapter Forty-one

'Well, now…' Kennedy said to the image of himself in the dressing-table mirror. 'If one were allowed to put two and two together and get five, our Dr Burgess has now been placed at the scene of the crime. Twice, in fact, if you consider the visit to Feng Shang.'

He sat with the notes on his lap, weighing it all up. Was he trapped by an illusion created by someone who wanted this murder pinned on Burgess?

Kennedy was reluctant to go too far down the road with the theory that Burgess murdered Berry. There was no ignoring the fact that Burgess had a seemingly cast-iron alibi.

With a fresh pot of tea reviving him, Kennedy set about re-examining the file containing the statements. He noticed something in Martin Shaw's statement that he had not remembered Martin telling him at the time of the questioning.

The statement read:

When we returned to Cumberland Basin for our first break, I decided to find out what – if anything – had been thrown into the canal earlier. I thought it may have been a rubbish bag and I was concerned that it might get caught up with our propeller – that could put us out of action for hours, if not the whole day. So, I wanted to find what was there.

The first thing I spotted was a rope with one end tied to a tree on the canal bank and the other end dangling in the canal. I hadn't seen that before – it wasn't used for the boats so I pulled it out of the water. It was quite long and I kept expecting to find something heavy on the end of it – that would have explained the splash. So, I kept pulling and pulling until it came out of the water. The only thing attached to the end of the rope was a large piece of canvas.

This was definitely not what had made the splash, so I threw the canvas on the bank and fetched a pole and started poking around in the bottom of the canal.

Kennedy wondered why Martin had not told him this at the time of the questioning. This oversight was his main preoccupation when there was a polite tapping on the door.

'Kennedy,' began the voice, 'have you done your homework yet? Are you coming out to play?'

Kennedy smiled, replaced the files and zig-zagged through the furniture to the door.

'Ah, well – that all depends on the games you want to play,' he said as he opened the door. He was saddened to find ann rea in her street clothes.

Chapter Forty-two

'So – did you get your story?'

They were on the outskirts of Grantchester, not a million miles from Cambridge. It hadn't taken ann rea and Kennedy long to pack up and pay their bills, separately, of course. Now they were enjoying their journey along the B-roads in the heart of the English countryside. They were looking for somewhere 'quaint' for a Sunday pub lunch and Grantchester looked like it might be just the place.

'I think I got enough for a decent article, but the sad thing is that most of the locals seem to prefer this time of the year, when the town is their own. Then there's little or no interference from tourists or outsiders,' ann rea answered.

'I can see that,' Kennedy said. 'Unless, of course, they managed to be in the breakfast-room this morning.'

'Kennedy, believe me – it was worth it just to see the look on your face… it was good to see… to see the human side of the great police-man,' she laughed.

Was this more encouragement or was he once again totally misreading the situation? Kennedy wondered if ann rea was considering this one of those famous platonic relationships, a relationship that a good – or bad – fifty percent of the partnership hated.

'Ah, this looks good,' she announced as they drove into Grantchester. 'What do you think?'

'Looks perfect to me,' he replied.

'What about that over there?' She nodded in the direction of a very quaint, typically English pub, guarded by two brightly painted stone lions. 'The Red Lion – will we try it?'

'I'm game.'

'I know that, Kennedy, but let's eat,' she laughed.

They found a parking space and entered the Red Lion where both enjoyed a traditional lunch in a not-too-crowded dining-room. Kennedy had a little wine, ann rea just a glass – after all, she was driving and she certainly didn't want to be nicked by a policeman.

'Let's take a stroll along the river,' she suggested. 'I'd like to walk off some of the food before getting back into the driving-seat again.'

'Good idea,' answered Kennedy, who happily would have walked back to London – any excuse to be in this fascinating woman's company for as long as possible. 'But you'd better wrap up well. I don't want your memory of this weekend to be one of you catching a cold.'

'Okay. I've a scarf in the car, I'll fetch that,' she replied.

The walkway along the riverside was very agreeable, although they had to cross a field to get to it, side-stepping signs that the cows had also eaten an enjoyable lunch. From spring to autumn, the area they walked through was packed with day-trippers, but today they shared the river with nothing more than the occasional boat going this way or that.

It was cold but the sky was unclouded and a flawless blue. They stopped at a lock-gate and watched for several minutes as the boats worked the locks, dropping down in level.

A beautiful new-looking cruiser stopped directly in front of them. The owner took his place at the top of the lock, tied his boat to the bank, leaving enough slack in the rope for the drop. He also left a long length of rope dangling from the bank to the boat. When the drop was completed, Kennedy tried to figure out how the sole occupant was going to get back up on to the now-high bank to untie his boat before moving on.

Kennedy was wondering whether or not he should offer to untie the boat, when the owner, on seeing that the lock-gates were now fully opened, pulled the unattached end of the rope. To Kennedy's amazement, the knot untied itself and the rope fell on to the deck of the boat which then continued its journey down the river.

'Amazing,' said Kennedy. 'And he used no mirrors, either.'

They both laughed.

'So, Kennedy, how did you get on with the Berry case this morning?'

'Well, I made a bit of progress.' Kennedy told ann rea about his conversation with the zoo worker.

'Hmm, and are you now convinced that Burgess is the murderer?'

Kennedy hesitated for a moment. 'It's illogical I know, but yes. I just have to work out how he did it and then, more importantly, why he did it. What his motive was.'

'Have you any ideas?' she inquired, as she slipped her arm through his. 'Any ideas at all?'

'No. Not unless his wife is lying and she really was having a scene with Berry. You know, a clever way to hide something is to put up a smokescreen, drawing attention away from what you're hiding.'

'Not possible, Kennedy. I told you – she and her partner are very, very happily in love. And what about his alibi? You told me that Burgess was on duty at the time of the murder.'

'Yeah, I know – I'm looking at that. I'm trying to see things from a totally different angle,' he replied.

They continued to walk in silence. He tightened his linked arm ever so slightly to try and move her closer to him, and then in his soft voice said, 'What about you ann rea? How long have you been alone?

'You're never alone with a mortgage, Kennedy,' she answered flippantly.

'Ah, come on – be serious.'

Kennedy thought that ann rea was either considering her answer or that she wasn't going to answer at all. But she did.

'Well, I don't like to talk about it, but I suppose I should. Yes, Kennedy, I was happily in love – very happily, indeed. I was all set to... to get married and live happily ever after and then he met someone else. I can't even say he was a shit about it. He was... he was a "good guy", as they say in the movies. He found someone else. I was so in love with him, I missed all the signs. But they were all there for me. He suddenly became not as interested, not as available. I even missed the major signal, "Let's have a trial separation." Lethal, fatal, final. He was trying to break it to me easily and I wasn't picking up on it and then he came right out... right out and said it. He told me he'd found someone else. He'd fallen in love with someone else.'

ann rea paused for a while. Kennedy said nothing. They walked in silence for a few moments.

'It destroyed me. I fell to pieces. You know, the usual story. I was very lucky; my landlord and landlady, Daniel and Lila Elliot, looked after me well at that point, treated me like a daughter. Eventually, I started to pick up the bits of my life again. I convinced myself that I had to protect myself so I started to work seriously at what I was doing. I set about trying to become a great journalist and I devoted myself to that. Yes, Kennedy, before you ask, there have been other men in my life but they haven't meant anything, availability is not an attraction for me. Love is not where you find it. Love is where it's hiding. You know, when you've been in love, and then you're not in love, you feel like you're never, ever going to be in love again and that hurts. That's what hurts the most.'

They stopped walking and she turned to face him. Keeping her linked arm in place, she slipped her other arm around his waist. Kennedy noticed a few tears had appeared in her eyes.

This was the first time that he had seen ann rea less than happy. He was annoyed at himself for asking the question that had produced this mood. He didn't know what to do, he felt helpless in this situation. It's easy to say meaningful, throw-away words when you didn't care , but Kennedy cared.

He held her closer to give her comfort, to take comfort. To give her strength, to take strength.

'Do you want to tell me about him?' was all Kennedy could say. He had a million other questions that he wanted to ask but that was the only one that would come out.

'Ah, another time perhaps, Kennedy.'

'I'm sorry, I didn't mean to…'

'Don't – no, Kennedy… it's okay. Honest, I was long overdue in telling someone about it. I'm glad you helped me get it out. After all,' she said, regaining her composure, 'what else are friends for?'

'I didn't think something so long ago could hurt so much,' he said.

ann rea gently broke free of him and took his hand. 'We'd better be heading back.'

They made their way back to the car. The moment had passed and one of the few things Kennedy had learned in his life was not to go chasing lost moments – there were too many of them.

Chapter Forty-three

The drive back to London was uneventful but friendly and soon ann rea was her usual self again. When they arrived outside Kennedy's house, she switched off the car and they sat in silence for a few minutes.

'Okay, Kennedy, I need one cup – just one cup, mind you – of your special tea. Then I'm going home; I'd like to do some work on the article tonight.'

'Great, no problem – no problem at all. It was fun and I had a great time. I even made some progress on my case. And if you want, I'll brew you a cup of tea that'll keep you on your article all night.'

'No alcohol, mind you.'

'In tea? Never, please.'

She felt comfortable in his house now and she wandered around his ground floor as he prepared his special brew. She asked him questions from the other rooms as she came across various objects and gadgets of interest.

She returned to the kitchen and gratefully accepted Kennedy's offering. 'Grannie! You weren't joking. Kennedy, what's in the tea?' ann rea exclaimed after her first mouthful.

'Ah, that would be telling, wouldn't it? And then you'd have no need to come back, would you?'

ann rea smiled at him. He took her free hand in his, he was becoming more confident now with body contact after their afternoon together.

'ann rea, is it okay if I kiss you?' Kennedy asked nervously.

Kennedy always felt awkward at this stage. You know each other quite well – you've been for dinner, lunch, movies, theatre, concert, a drink, whatever. But you want to move the relationship on to another level – the next level. At the same time, you care about the person, so you don't want to use your friendship or closeness to compromise them.

Kennedy believed in confronting the situation head on, as it were. None of the clumsiness of trying to slide up to her on the sofa, manoeuvring his arm around her shoulders in the hope that she wouldn't notice until it was in position. Then trying to ensure that your mouths are, at the precise moment, within homing distance of each other. Nothing can cure the awfulness you feel if she strategically misses your mouth while saying, Great painting, or What's that book? or You like hideous green things as well? How wonderful, so do I. Anything to start a conversation. Anything rather than taking that step.

Now he could wait no longer. Kennedy was prepared to risk rejection.

'ann rea, is it okay if I kiss you?' The words echoed around his brain over and over again.

'Yes, Kennedy, yes. It was okay to kiss me ages ago. I was beginning to wonder about you.'

'But I thought… I thought the time wasn't right. I didn't want to ruin anything by rushing it,' he declared, painfully aware of his clumsiness.

'The time has long been right for kissing, Kennedy… but not for making love. Nowadays, too many people think that a kiss is an invitation and an acceptance to the epilogue. I prefer to work my way through the book chapter by chapter.'

'I love kissing…' was all Kennedy could think to say.

'So, are we going to get down to it or are we going to discuss the pros and cons of kissing all night? I was hoping…'

Kennedy pulled her gently towards him. ann rea's eyes had such a wonderful way of smiling. That was the last thing he saw, her smiling eyes, as he closed his a few seconds before their lips met.

ann rea's lips were so soft – fluid, silky, delicate, gentle. Her mouth was inviting – pleasing, sweet, sensitive. Her tongue caressed his, coaxing before venturing into his mouth. Her tongue fondled his teeth.

Blood was exploding in distant parts of his body. He was breathless but desperate not to break off this kiss simply to catch some air. His head was dizzy. He opened his eyes for a second to look at her face, or the part of her face he could see – her closed eyelids.

He desperately wanted to kiss her eyelids, perhaps he'd do so later. This current exploration was far too pleasurable to interrupt. He played with her tongue, catching it delicately between his teeth and then caressing if softly with his own tongue.

Now he could feel the fullness of her body pressed against his. When he felt he may have been a little forceful with his kissing, he reduced the pressure so that their lips were gently petting – like feathers touching airily as they fall in the breeze.

Kennedy felt like he was falling. ann rea was building up the pressure again, each time exciting him with something anew. This was a pure kiss, lacking in sexual hunger.

It was the closest Kennedy had been to ann rea and she smelt beautiful, fresh and alive. She'd been out all day, eaten a meal, drank tea and wine but her mouth tasted mint-fresh. For one split second, Kennedy wondered what his own mouth tasted like, but only for one split second.

The kiss continued timelessly. They drank the waters of each other's mouth, neither wanting the kiss to end.

But end it did.

In movie terms, it was a long fade with their lips just brushing each other. When eventually their lips did separate, Kennedy kissed each of ann rea's closed eyelids.

They continued to hug each other. Kennedy and ann rea didn't talk. There was no need to talk, no use for words. They rocked gently, hugging for some minutes.

'I've got to go home, Kennedy,' she said quietly.

'I know,' he replied and he helped her on with her coat and took her out to the car.

'Speak to you tomorrow,' ann rea said as she kissed her fingers and placed them on Kennedy's lips.

Chapter Forty-four

On his way to the office the following morning, Kennedy stopped off at Regent's Bookshop in Parkway and asked for something on knots. Peter, the ever reliable bookseller had two such books in stock – *This is the Colour Book of Knots* by Floris Hin and *The Complete Guide to Knots* by Mario Bigon and Guido Regazloni. Kennedy recognised the second title – he'd seen the same book in Burgess' study. He paid the eight pounds and ninety-nine pence and returned to his office.

Kennedy settled down behind his desk with his second cup of tea of the day and his newly acquired book. He browsed through it, not finding what he was after. He decided to re-read it more thoroughly.

Twenty minutes elapsed before he discovered exactly what he had been searching for. The knot in question was the Highwayman's Hitch, also known as a Draw Hitch. It was the featured knot on pages sixty-four and sixty-five of this now very valuable book.

Content with his work, he placed another piece of paper on the case noticeboard. All he had to do now was work out the motive. Kennedy revised the information he had on Dr Berry, the information he had gained from his meeting with Sheila Berry. This turned up nothing new so he moved on to his notes concerning Burgess and his wife.

Kennedy wondered if Amelia Burgess' lover could in some way be involved in this plot. Kennedy had not questioned her or even tried to find out anything about her. Had this been a mistake?

There were so many things going around his head, thanks to his productive time at the hotel. His mind returned to that eventful Sunday with ann rea. Pleasant thoughts though they were, Kennedy knew that, should he continue with them, he'd make no further progress on the case.

Time for a change of scene. He collected his coat from behind the door and headed off into the chilly morning.

Kennedy stood at the gate to North Bridge House for several moments trying to decide which way to go. His feet made the choice for him and five minutes later he arrived at Cumberland Basin. He spent a considerable amount of time trying to reconstruct the sequence of events that had taken place there on the morning of Berry's death.

Kennedy felt sure that he'd worked out exactly what had happened on that darkened morning but he still needed to discover the *why* of the case. He walked around the basin at street level and, as much as he could, at canal level.

'You're very clever, mister – very clever. But I'll catch you,' Kennedy said to the canal. He threw in a stone and, before the ripples had died away, turned to walk back to his office.

Now Kennedy felt he was focused enough to return to his review of the case. He removed all the files relating to Norman Collins and William Jackson. A mistake, perhaps, but should he be proven wrong in his hunch, he could always return to them.

One of Kennedy's main strengths as a policeman was that he was not scared of being wrong. He didn't sit on the fence. He'd have an opinion on a matter and would act on it until such time as he, or someone else, proved his opinion wrong. At that point, he would start all over again. But he was always prepared to get on with it.

A couple of hours had passed and turned up nothing new. During that time, there had been interruptions from Irvine, who was cajoled into preparing a fresh pot of tea, and from Coles, who just wanted to see if there was anything she could do.

The posse were all of the opinion that Kennedy was about to crack the Berry case. He'd 'gone quiet' on them and that was a usual sign.

Kennedy wished he was as close to cracking it as they seemed to think he was.

He liked – no, he insisted – on offering a full and final solution to all his cases. He didn't like leaving the burden of proof to the judge and jury. Who said that a jury was always going to get it right? It's a powerful-sounding name, but a jury only consisted of twelve mere humans. Twelve people with their own problems – financial worries, moving to bigger and more expensive houses, work problems, bad health, wives and husbands being unfaithful, troublesome children. Kennedy often marvelled at how people, with so many burdens of their own, could clear their mind and concentrate on the non-stop parade of boring, badly presented evidence. The system encouraged them to view the suspect uncritically – never mind that the lawyers had them carefully dressed and rehearsed for their appearance in court. What about the victim? If only the jury could see the victim at the time of the death, and the destruction and disintegration of the victim's relatives. If, just once, the jury could go beyond the grave so that the victim could tell their side of the story.

No, much too scary to leave it to a jury, thought Kennedy. He preferred to have proof – proof that left absolutely no doubt in the minds of judge or jury as to who committed the crime and why.

And why?

But – and it was a very big but – he felt he was a long way from such a breakthrough. He felt sure that whoever committed this crime was not going to come running with his hands outstretched, begging for handcuffs, saying, Fair cop, guv, I did it. Kennedy thought that this particular murderer was going to be tricky to catch. No point in being brainy if you can't show off just a little bit, was how Kennedy felt his suspect would think. No, he was going to have to catch this one and catch him in such a way as to leave no room for retreat.

Chapter Forty-five

Naught, nil, zilch. Two days later and he was no nearer to solving the puzzle. Totally frustrating. Kennedy visited Sheila Berry, who was doing what a good person in her position would do – getting on with her life in the best way possible under the circumstances.

He discussed the case with Superintendent Castle, who was, as usual, completely understanding and supportive.

But it was left to ann rea to be the light in his life during those two dark days.

'Kennedy,' she began, as they sat down to dine in NB Restaurant, in Princess Road. 'What happens when, like in this Berry Case, the investigation grinds to a halt with the case still unsolved? If nothing new turns up, will they take you off it and put you on something else?'

'Well, it would depend,' he began. 'The Super would call me in for an appraisal of the case. He would make a decision based on the information I had just given him, assessing the current work-load and the likelihood of the case being successfully solved.'

'So, would that case still remain in your file or is there a special place for unsolved crimes?' she asked.

'You mean, like a home in Worthing?' he laughed.

'I'm serious, Kennedy,' she chastised.

'Sorry. No, it would stay with me so that, should there be any new breaks or updates in information, I'd be best qualified to see how it changed the big picture,' he answered.

'How long would it remain an unsolved case? Do they ever close an unsolved case?'

'No, they never close a case these days. It's entered on the computer under different headings and can be cross-referenced with other cases in the future, just in case they link up or are in some way connected.'

'I sense a story here, Kennedy… or even a series, don't you think? How would I find out about these cases?'

'I don't really know. I suppose you could approach the Super or the press office. If you presented your idea to them in the right way, you might be in with a chance,' Kennedy replied.

'You think they'd go for it, then?' ann rea quizzed.

'Well, I suppose some publicity for some of these old cases might be good. You may trigger somebody's memory and bring in some new relevant leads. Or you could even reach witnesses who missed the coverage first time around, because of holidays or whatever. It could be good, ann rea. It could help to rid us of some of the unsolved files. But you need to approach it that way; not, Look at all these cases your local police have failed to solve. Don't do that and it could be good,' he said encouragingly.

'Yes, I can see that. I think I'll try and convince the editor that it would make a fascinating piece and let me make a series out of it. I'll make a couple of calls tomorrow,' she smiled.

Kennedy got stuck into his tuna fish bake and ann rea tucked into her vegetable strudel – as ever, both were delicious.

Kennedy lowered his knife and fork to the table and took a sip of his cold, crisp white wine. He was terrible at remembering the names of wine, the vintages and the whole palaver but, fortunately, the waiter-cum-owner knew exactly what Kennedy liked and didn't make a fuss serving it.

'ann rea,' Kennedy began, as the wine washed down his last mouthful of food. 'About this friendship thing, I must admit I'm quite getting into it, particularly after the weekend.'

ann rea smiled.

'So, I was wondering – what happens next?' Before she could answer, he quickly took another mouthful of wine.

'I bet you were, Kennedy. Look, I like you and not as in, I *only* like you. The more I know you, the more I like you and the more I want to know you more. I want to be sure, Kennedy. I want to take time… take time to make sure it's right. I want you to desire me, Kennedy. If we get together, I need you to look at me the way you looked at me on Sunday in the hotel…'

Kennedy smiled as the memory flashed before him.

'I want to have romance. I don't want to get into a relationship with you where I take you – or your pot belly, or your Ghandi shorts, or your spilt toothpaste, or your shaving-gear lying around – as part of the deal. I don't want you taking me lying around, or vegetating, or dressing badly, or wearing careless make-up, or stale underwear, and so on, as part of the package. If we get it together, Kennedy, it has to be forever. If not, I'm not interested.'

'I don't have a pot belly, do I?'

'No, of course not. And I don't want you to, either. I want you always to be as attractive and as fresh to me as you are at this moment. I want to keep that, Kennedy; I need to keep that. I want you to always want to get to know me more. I want always to want to know more about you. I don't want to reach the stage where we meet for five minutes at the end of each day, jump on each other's bones at the weekend and spend hours on Sundays with each other, sitting in complete silence, me reading the Sundays, you off in your own world. If we get together, I want us to be together.'

Kennedy made as though to speak. But he could see that ann rea hadn't finished, so he took another sip of wine.

'We may, or we may not, make love. Don't you like that mystery, that romance? I don't know if it will happen, Kennedy. I don't know and I don't want to know until it does happen – or not, as the case may be. And if we should make love, I don't want either of us to take it for granted that it will ever happen again. That way – hopefully – if it does happen again, it'll be just as magical as the first time.'

She smiled and her eyes warmed his heart and turned his knees to jelly. Kennedy took another gulp of wine.

'So, Kennedy – you're the other half of this duo. How do you feel about it? How do you feel now you know my dreams?'

'You don't ask little questions, do you? All right, I'll tell you: I've never, ever, known anyone like you during my life. I wasn't looking for anyone and then you came along and you... you became so important to me. And I feel great about it. It's like you came from nowhere and now you're my best friend and, if I'm honest, I think that if we start from friendship we might have a chance. But most of all, I think it's going to be fun hanging out together.'

'Okay, cool.' She lifted her glass. 'To friends and to fun. We never need discuss it again. Let's not talk about what's going to happen, let's just let it happen, eh?'

'Friends and fun!' Kennedy said, as he helped himself to another drink of wine. 'And forever,' he said under his breath.

'I'll drop you off on my way home, Kennedy. I want to do some work on this unsolved crimes thing.'

'Good,' he said, looking at his watch. 'I'll be home in time to see *Northern Exposure*.'

Chapter Forty-six

'Shit!' Kennedy shouted at the top of his voice. It was early the following morning and he was in his office, engrossed in the Berry case files, taking advantage of the rare quietness of North Bridge House.

Irvine, responding to the noise, ran into the office with panic in his eyes.

Kennedy was grinning from ear to ear. 'It's here, it's all here. It's been here all the time,' he exclaimed.

The detective sergeant continued to stare at Kennedy, hoping for an explanation. Kennedy's eyes remained transfixed on the file before him.

'I've been checking through the rosters that we collected from Staff Nurse Butler, God bless her cotton socks. I wanted to check the time Burgess had come on duty on Wednesday 20th January. I was also interested in the time he spent on duty during the next forty-eight hours. I was trying to find some connection between Burgess and Berry and I had a hunch it might have something to do with Susanne Collins' death.'

Irvine was on the edge of his proverbial seat.

'So, I wanted to find out how soon after the death of Susanne Collins our Dr Burgess would have learnt about Dr Berry's problem. One of my suspicions was that maybe Burgess discovered the facts and was blackmailing Berry. I wondered if Berry was about to admit what had happened – via his appointment with his solicitor – thus exposing Burgess as a blackmailer. In that case, Burgess would have been forced to murder Berry so as to avoid being exposed. But no – it's much simpler than that, Jimmy. It's been here all the time, and I missed it. I made a fatal mistake – I made an assumption and carried on with the investigation based on that false assumption.'

'What was that, sir? What on earth have you found?' Excitement was getting the better of Irvine.

'Well, I assumed that Berry was the doctor on duty when Susanne Collins was admitted to the hospital. This assumption was easily made, Berry *was* the doctor on duty when Susanne Collins died. But Burgess was on duty when Susanne Collins was admitted.'

'So, it was Burgess – not Berry – who made the wrong diagnosis on Susanne Collins,' returned Irvine, as the penny dropped.

'Yes, Jimmy, Dr Spencer Burgess made the false diagnosis that led to the death of Susanne Collins. Motive – that's his motive – that's what's been missing. I'm pretty sure I know how he did it. I just didn't know *why* he did it. Obviously, Berry knew that Burgess was the one who'd made the mistake – that's clearly what had been troubling him – obviously the point of the scheduled appointment with his solicitor,' Kennedy speculated.

'You're right, you're absolutely one-hundred-percent correct,' the detective sergeant gasped.

Kennedy's mind was racing. 'If the true circumstances of the Susanne Collins situation came out, it would have dealt a death-blow to Burgess' illustrious career – the end of his promotion line. He couldn't have afforded Berry telling the truth.'

'But why didn't all this come out in the hospital report?' inquired Irvine.

'Good point. Our friend, Alexander Bowles, has a few more questions to answer. Let's check his statement.'

Kennedy rummaged around his desk for a few moments until he found the statement and proceeded to read.

'Clever, very clever. But I should have noticed it,' Kennedy smiled to himself. He could afford to now that he had solved the case. 'Look here, at the beginning of the report, when he's referring to the "admitting-doctor", he acknowledges him merely as the "doctor". But by the time we reach the end of the report, the doctor in attendance is referred to as Dr Berry.'

Kennedy rose from his chair. 'Let's go round and see Mr Bowles, shall we? No, even better, why don't you send someone down to the hospital and bring him in for questioning. And have a separate car pick up Burgess, bring him in, as well. But we'll let him stew for a bit, shall we?'

No sooner said than done.

Thirty-seven minutes later, the very same Alexander Bowles was seated before Kennedy and his sergeant.

'So,' began Kennedy in his soft voice, 'you weren't exactly forthcoming with the truth last time we spoke, were you, Mr Bowles?'

'I didn't tell you any lies, Inspector Kennedy.'

'Maybe not, but I'm sure I could make a charge of "obstructing the police while in the course of their duty" stick.'

'How so, Inspector?'

Kennedy looked at the ceiling and breathed a large sigh, a very large sigh.

'Well, sir,' Irvine cut in, 'while in the course of our duty to apprehend the murderer of Dr Edmund Berry, you intentionally withheld information from us and distorted the truth. You, in your own way, have helped hide the identity of the murderer. I'm afraid we hold a very dim view on such actions.'

'But I told you all I knew at the time,' answered Bowles, clearly stalling in an attempt to find out the extent of their knowledge.

'Can we keep the bullshit to a minimum, please?' snapped Kennedy, moving in until his nose was about three inches from the no-longer proud hooter of Alexander Bowles.

Bowles wasn't used to this treatment.

'I'll spell it out for you, Mr Bowles. One – you knew that Burgess was the doctor on duty and the admitting-doctor of Susanne Collins. Two – you knew that, because he incorrectly diagnosed the illness, his treatment or lack of proper treatment – his sin of omission – led to the untimely death a few days later of Ms Collins.'

Kennedy paused to allow Bowles to realise the game was up.

'Three – you also knew that, because Berry was the doctor attending Susanne Collins at the time of her death, it was he – and not Burgess – who incorrectly took the blame for her death.

'Four – I also believe that, because you were party to the above information, you were also aware that Dr Burgess most probably murdered Dr Berry to keep this information secret.

'Five…' Kennedy had raised four fingers and now raised his thumb, 'You are responsible for the fact that Mrs Sheila Berry is now a widow and young Sam Berry is fatherless. You're responsible for the fact the Susanne Collins' father and brother are now grieving.'

Kennedy changed hands.

'Six …'

Kennedy was now shouting.

'I think you're a complete shit and you make me sick, utterly sick.'

But Bowles didn't know when to give in. 'My job, Inspector, is to look after the interests of the hospital…'

'At the expense of people's lives? My job is to make people like you aware that there are no "acceptable losses" – there will be no "limiting of liability". You will – one way or another – pay for your sins.'

Bowles was starting to look severely uncomfortable. His top lip and forehead were leaking sweat.

'Look,' he said, 'I thought that Dr Burgess had probably made a genuine mistake and by the time it had come to my attention, most of the storm had settled down. I can't believe that you have any evidence that Burgess could have killed Berry. He was on duty that morning, he couldn't have killed him. I assumed, like everyone else – everyone else except you, that is – that Dr Berry had committed suicide. I became slightly suspicious when Dr Burgess refused to discuss the matter with me. I then began to worry but thought, what good could it do to,' said Bowles, desperate although subdued as the enormity of the Collins and Berry deaths sank in.

'The truth must come out if Susanne Collins' and Dr Berry's families are to start to lay their loved ones' memories to rest. They must try to put their lives in order. That's what good it would have done.'

Kennedy had nothing more to say to Bowles.

'Oh, take him away, put him somewhere and I'll decide what to do with him later,' he commanded.

Chapter Forty-seven

'Okay – bring him to the interrogation room immediately. I'll meet you there, Jimmy.' Kennedy was speaking through the intercom to Irvine.

'Yes, Dr Burgess. Please come in and sit down,' Kennedy gestured.

'I hope you realise that I'm a busy man, and hospitals do not run themselves. First, Mr Bowles and now myself,' Burgess huffed indignantly.

'Dr Burgess – I think the hospital is going to have to do without you for quite some time,' Kennedy replied patiently.

'What on earth are you on about? What's this all about?'

'Oh – I think you know, Doctor. But let's pretend you don't know. Let's play the game your way. Why don't you just sit there, keep quiet, and I'll do all the talking. I'll tell you exactly what happened. Then perhaps – if it's not too much trouble – we can have a chat at the end. Okay?' Kennedy offered.

Burgess merely shrugged his shoulders.

This isn't going to be easy, Irvine's eyes said to Kennedy across the table.

Kennedy offered Burgess a cup of tea. He refused without words and Kennedy poured himself another cup. He returned to his chair and tried to make himself comfortable.

'Now, where do I begin?' Kennedy answered his own question. 'Oh, yes – at the beginning. Around lunch time on Wednesday 20th January this year, a Susanne Collins was brought into the Accident and Emergency Department at St Pancras All Saints Hospital. You were the doctor on duty.'

Burgess arched his eyebrows but resisted the temptation to speak. Kennedy continued: 'You examined her. Ms Collins had a swollen leg, she couldn't bear to stand on it. She also had a slight temperature. You, Dr Burgess, concluded that she was suffering from Phlebitis, which is an inflammation of the vein. You prescribe antibiotics in the form of Ampicillin; four injections a day, I believe. You admitted her to hospital for observation, I believe – and to ensure the swelling went down. The next day, Thursday 21st January, the swelling has not receded so you keep her on antibiotics. Late the following day, Friday 22nd January, Ms Collins takes a turn for the worse. She's having trouble breathing and complains of chest pains. The duty-doctor on Friday 22nd January is, in fact, Dr Berry. Dr Berry, after examining Ms Collins, gives her a Diamorphine injection to ease the pain. Dr Berry realises your diagnosis was incorrect and that Ms Collins is not suffering from Phlebitis but, in fact, has a blood clot in her leg.'

Burgess sat rigid, his face showing no emotion.

'The blood clot has, by this time, travelled from her leg and is close to her heart. Ms Collins becomes unconscious and Dr Berry puts her on a Heparin drip in the hope of dissolving the blood clot. Unfortunately, he's too late and Ms Collins dies. Berry is held responsible for the death of Ms Collins but he knows that you, Dr Burgess – and you alone – were responsible. The only other person who has this information is your good friend, Mr Bowles. You persuade Bowles that to protect himself and the hospital's name, he must keep quiet about it. You then decide that Dr Berry has to die in order to keep your secret safe. However, you didn't want something as ordinary as an accidental death to put an end to your promotion plans...'

'You seem to forget, Inspector,' interrupted Burgess, who had been paying very close attention to Kennedy's monologue, 'that I was on duty the morning Dr Berry fell in the canal.'

'I did say you would have a chance at the end. Please bear with me, Doctor.'

Burgess sat back in his chair.

'On Friday 29th January, you dined at the Feng Shang Restaurant. This restaurant, as you know, overlooks the Cumberland Basin. As you dined, you were fine-tuning your plan to murder Dr Berry. On Monday 1st February, Berry dines with his family at home at four o'clock in the afternoon. He leaves his house at five-forty-five and travels to the hospital where he is on call from six o'clock that afternoon till two o'clock the following morning. He watches the BBC *Nine O'clock News* and retires to his cot at about ten o'clock. That's the last time he is seen alive. You, Dr Burgess, went off duty at one o'clock on the same afternoon and, in the early hours of the following morning – Tuesday 2nd February – you slipped into Dr Berry's room and injected alcohol directly into his bloodstream.

'You injected him between the toes – this was the most convenient place to inject somebody sleeping without disturbing them. Also, injection marks are unlikely to show up there during the autopsy examination. Dr Berry was now unconscious with alcohol and you lifted him into a wheelchair. You wheeled him out to the hospital car-park and loaded him and the wheelchair into the back of your Range Rover. You then drove to the Outer Circle in Regent's park, near St Mark's Bridge and the Cumberland Basin. You were spotted at this location, wheeling Dr Berry in the direction of the bridge at 4.30am.'

Kennedy noticed the first twitch from Burgess. After a mouthful of tea, he continued.

'You also removed from the back of the Range Rover a piece of old canvas and two pieces of rope – one a lot longer than the other. You throw the longer rope and the canvas over the side of St Mark's Bridge to land on the canal pathway below. The remaining rope, you tie around Berry's chest, just under his arms, thus explaining the marks that were found in the autopsy examination. You lower him down on to the canal pathway by slowly using a braking device of wrapping the rope around the knob on the bridge side, letting it down hand-over-hand. The rope left marks and rope hairs on the knob. Keeping the rope in the same position, you lower yourself down on to the pathway. You then move the comatose body down the canal bank, away from the bridge and further into the basin. You place the body on the canvas and out of sight behind some rubbish. And now for the complicated bit, Dr Burgess.'

Kennedy felt that some of Burgess' aloofness had evaporated.

'You attach one end of the long rope to the canvas that Berry is lying on. You then tie the rope about one third the way along its length to the side rail of the Sailing Diamond. You use a Highwayman's Hitch – you'll remember it, I'm sure, Dr Burgess – it's on page sixty-four of *The Complete Guide to Knots*. There's a copy of it in your study which you may like to consult – if you ever get home again. Now, the magic of this knot, as you know, is that if you pull the "working" end of the rope, the knot will hold firm and take the strain. But if you pull the "loose" end of the rope, the knot will become completely undone.'

Kennedy removed a piece of thin rope from his pocket and demonstrated the knot on the back of his chair.

He went on, again using the rope to demonstrate.

'Next, you tie the long end, or "loose" end of the rope to a tree on the bank. You then hide the rope along the hedge-growth and in the water. Finally, you climb up the other rope back onto the bridge, pack up the rope in the back of your car and return to the hospital. All this climbing and pulling and lowering takes its toll on your body and you put your back out. It must have been serious because you are still suffering from it when I visit you for the first time a few days later. You return to the hospital in time for your duty-call at 6am. At 7am, Mr Martin Shaw and his colleague ready the Sailing Diamond for its first journey of the day. As they cast off, the "working" section of the rope – stretched between the boat and the canvas – becomes taut and the boat pulls the canvas and Dr Berry's body into the canal. The point of the canvas is so you don't have the tell-tale rope tied to Dr Berry's body. Martin Shaw heard the splash but he didn't see anything apart from a few air bubbles. The "loose" section of the rope between the tree and the rail on the Sailing Diamond now starts to become taut and the tension unties the Highwayman's Hitch on the rail. The Sailing Diamond sails off, unaware of the intrigue left in its path. Dr Berry is still unconscious from the alcohol and drowns in the muddy water of the canal while you are busy collecting your perfect alibi on duty at the hospital.'

Kennedy drew a breath.

'Very, very nearly the perfect crime and it would have been were it not for the total commitment Sheila Berry had for the memory of her husband,' Kennedy concluded.

Burgess could only bow his head, stunned, shocked, silenced. As far as he was concerned, though, he was only guilty of one crime – the crime of being found out.

'Take him away, DS Irvine, and charge him with murder.'

Chapter Forty-eight

Kennedy returned to his office and made a fresh pot of tea. He drank it slowly, studying his case noticeboard – it looked different to him now – now that the case was solved. His thoughts were not ones of satisfaction for 'breaking' the case but instead they were with Sheila and Sam Berry – and with Norman Collins and his father.

Kennedy's phone rang. He let it ring a few times before saying out loud, 'Oh, well, here we go again. Another case.'

He lifted the phone.

'Kennedy?'

'Hi, ann rea.'

Kennedy gave her the news.

'Brilliant, well done. Dinner tonight? You can tell me all the twists and turns.'

'Yes, great.'

'My place or yours?'

'Yours,' he replied.

'Good. I'll pick you up at North Bridge House at seven. Kennedy, you bring the wine.'

'Great, okay. Oh, ann rea…'

'We'll talk tonight, Kennedy, see you then.'

Chapter Forty-nine

Kennedy turned over on the bed.
'ann rea?' His voice was sleepy.
'What is it, Kennedy?'
'ann rea, can we make love again?'
'Kennedy!' she replied breathily.
'Hmm?'
'We only just made love!'
'Okay, right – I just wanted to make sure I wasn't dreaming.'

BLOODLINES the cutting-edge crime and mystery imprint...

I Love The Sound of Breaking Glass by Paul Charles

First outing for Irish-born Detective Inspector Christy Kennedy whose beat is Camden Town, north London. Peter O'Browne, managing director of Camden Town Records, is missing. Is his disappearance connected with a mysterious fire that ravages his north London home? And just who was using his credit card in darkest Dorset?

Although up to his neck in other cases, Detective Inspector Christy Kennedy and his team investigate, plumbing the hidden depths of London's music industry, turning up murder, chart-rigging scams, blackmail and worse. *I Love The Sound of Breaking Glass* is a detective story with a difference. Part whodunnit, part howdunnit and part love story, it features a unique method of murder, a plot with more twists and turns than the road from Kingsmarkham to St Mary Mead.

Paul Charles is one of Europe's best known music promoters and agents. In this, his stunning début, he reveals himself as master of the crime novel. ISBN 1 899344 16 0 – £7

Perhaps She'll Die! by John B Spencer

Giles could never say 'no' to a woman... any woman. But when he tangled with Celeste, he made a mistake... A bad mistake.

Celeste was married to Harry, and Harry walked a dark side of the street that Giles – with his comfortable lifestyle and fashionable media job – could only imagine in his worst nightmares. And when Harry got involved in nightmares, people had a habit of getting hurt.

Set against the boom and gloom of Eighties Britain, *Perhaps She'll Die!* is classic *noir* with a centre as hard as toughened diamond.
ISBN 1 899344 14 4 – £5.99

Quake City by John B Spencer

The third novel to feature Charley Case, the hard-boiled investigator of a future that follows the 'Big One of Ninety-Seven' – the quake that literally rips California apart and makes LA an Island.

'Classic Chandleresque private eye tale, jazzed up by being set in the future... but some things never change – PI Charley Case still has trouble with women and a trusty bottle of bourbon is always at hand. An entertaining addition to the private eye canon.' – *Mail on Sunday*
ISBN 1 899344 02 0 – £5.99

BLOODLINES the cutting-edge crime and mystery imprint...

The Hackman Blues by Ken Bruen

'If Martin Amis was writing crime novels, this is what he would hope to write.' – *Books in Ireland*

'...I haven't taken my medication for the past week. If I couldn't go a few days without the lithium, I was in deep shit. I'd gotten the job ten days earlier and it entailed a whack of pub-crawling. Booze and medication is the worst of songs. Sing that!

A job of pure simplicity. Find a white girl in Brixton. Piece of cake. What I should have done is doubled my medication and lit a candle to St Jude – maybe a lot of candles.'

Add to the mixture a lethal ex-con, an Irish builder obsessed with Gene Hackman, the biggest funeral Brixton has ever seen, and what you get is the Blues like they've never been sung before.

Ken Bruen's powerful second novel is a gritty and grainy mix of crime noir and Urban Blues that greets you like a mugger stays with you like a razor-scar.

GQ described his début novel as:

'The most startling and original crime novel of the decade.'

The Hackman Blues is Ken Bruen's best novel yet.

Fresh Blood II edited by Mike Ripley & Maxim Jakubowski

Follow-up to the highly-acclaimed original volume (see below), featuring short stories from John Baker, Christopher Brookmyre, Ken Bruen, Carol Anne Davis, Christine Green, Lauren Henderson, Charles Higson, Maxim Jakubowski, Phil Lovesey, Mike Ripley, Iain Sinclair, John Tilsley, John Williams, and RD Wingfield (Inspector Frost).

Fresh Blood edited by Mike Ripley & Maxim Jakubowski

Featuring the cream of the British New Wave of crime writers including John Harvey, Mark Timlin, Chaz Brenchley, Russell James, Stella Duffy, Ian Rankin, Nicholas Blincoe, Joe Canzius, Denise Danks, John B Spencer, Graeme Gordon, and a previously unpublished extract from the late Derek Raymond. Includes an introduction from each author explaining their views on crime fiction in the '90s and a comprehensive foreword on the genre from Angel-creator, Mike Ripley. ISBN 1 899344 03 9 – £6.99

BLOODLINES the cutting-edge crime and mystery imprint...

That Angel Look by Mike Ripley

'The outrageous, rip-roarious Mr Ripley is an abiding delight...'
– Colin Dexter

A chance encounter (in a pub, of course) lands street-wise, cab-driving Angel the ideal job as an all-purpose assistant to a trio of young and very sexy fashion designers.

But things are nowhere near as straightforward as they should be and it soon becomes apparent that no-one is telling the truth – least of all Angel! Double-cross turns to triple-cross and Angel finds himself set-up by friend and enemy alike. This time, Angel could really meet his match...

'I never read Ripley on trains, planes or buses. He makes me laugh and it annoys the other passengers.' – Minette Walters.

1 899344 23 3 – £8

Shrouded by Carol Anne Davis

Douglas likes women — quiet women; the kind he deals with at the mortuary where he works. Douglas meets Marjorie, unemployed, gaining weight and losing confidence. She talks and laughs a lot to cover up her shyness, but what Douglas really needs is a lover who'll stay still — deadly still. Driven by lust and fear, Douglas finds a way to make girls remain excitingly silent and inert. But then he is forced to blank out the details of their unplanned deaths.

Perhaps only Marjorie can fulfil his growing sexual hunger. If he could just get her into a state of limbo. Douglas studies his textbooks to find a way...

Shrouded is a powerful and accomplished début, tautly-plotted, dangerously erotic and vibrating with tension and suspense.

ISBN 1 899344 17 9— £7

Smalltime by Jerry Raine

Smalltime is a taut, psychological crime thriller, set among the seedy world of petty criminals and no-hopers. In this remarkable début, Jerry Raine shows just how easily curiosity can turn into fear amid the horrors, despair and despondency of life lived a little too near the edge.

'Jerry Raine's Smalltime carries the authentic whiff of sleazy Nineties Britain. He vividly captures the world of stunted ambitions and their evil consequences.' – Simon Brett

'The first British contemporary crime novel featuring an underclass which no one wants. Absolutely authentic and quite possibly important.'– Philip Oakes, Literary Review. ISBN 1 899344 13 6 – £5.99

Outstanding Paperback Fiction from The Do-Not Press:

Elvis – The Novel by Robert Graham, Keith Baty

'Quite simply, the greatest music book ever written'
	– Mick Mercer, *Melody Maker*

The everyday tale of an imaginary superstar eccentric. The Presley neither his fans nor anyone else knew. First-born of triplets, he came from the backwoods of Tennessee. Driven by a burning ambition to sing opera, Fate sidetracked him into creating Rock 'n' roll.

His classic movie, *Driving A Sportscar Down To A Beach In Hawaii* didn't win the Oscar he yearned for, but The Beatles revived his flagging spirits, and he stunned the world with a guest appearance in Batman.

Further shockingly momentous events have led him to the peaceful, contented lifestyle he enjoys today.

'Books like this are few and far between.' – Charles Shaar Murray, *NME*
ISBN 1 899344 19 5 – £7

The Users by Brian Case

The welcome return of Brian Case's brilliantly original '60s cult classic.
'A remarkable debut' –Anthony Burgess

'Why Case's spiky first novel from 1968 should have languished for nearly thirty years without a reprint must be one of the enigmas of modern publishing. Mercilessly funny and swaggeringly self-conscious, it could almost be a template for an early Martin Amis.' – *Sunday Times*.
ISBN 1 899344 05 5– £5.99

Charlie's Choice: The First Charlie Muffin Omnibus by Brian Freemantle – *Charlie Muffin; Clap Hands, Here Comes Charlie; The Inscrutable Charlie Muffin*

Charlie Muffin is not everybody's idea of the ideal espionage agent. Dishevelled, cantankerous and disrespectful, he refuses to play by the Establishment's rules. Charlie's axiom is to screw anyone from anywhere to avoid it happening to him. But it's not long before he finds himself offered up as an unwilling sacrifice by a disgraced Department, desperate to win points in a ruthless Cold War. Now for the first time, the first three Charlie Muffin books are collected together in one volume.

'Charlie is a marvellous creation' – *Daily Mail*

Also available in paperback from The Do-Not Press

Dancing With Mermaids
by Miles Gibson

'Absolutely first rate. Absolutely wonderful' – Ray Bradbury

Strange things are afoot in the Dorset fishing town of Rams Horn.

Set close to the poisonous swamps at the mouth of the River Sheep, the town has been isolated from its neighbours for centuries.

But mysterious events are unfolding… A seer who has waited for years for her drowned husband to reappear is haunted by demons, an African sailor arrives from the sea and takes refuge with a widow and her idiot daughter. Young boys plot sexual crimes and the doctor, unhinged by his desire for a woman he cannot have, turns to a medicine older than his own.

'An imaginative tour de force and a considerable stylistic achievement.
When it comes to pulling one into a world of his own making, Gibson
has few equals among his contemporaries.'
– *Time Out*
'A wild, poetic exhalation that sparkles and hoots and flies.'
– *The New Yorker*
'An extraordinary talent dances with perfect control
across hypnotic page.' – *Financial Times*

ISBN 1 899344 25 X – £7

The Sandman
by Miles Gibson

"I am the Sandman. I am the butcher in soft rubber gloves. I am the acrobat called death.
I am the fear in the dark. I am the gift of sleep…"

Growing up in a small hotel in a shabby seaside town, Mackerel Burton has no idea that he is to grow up to become a slick and ruthless serial killer. A lonely boy, he amuses himself by perfecting his conjuring tricks, but slowly the magic turns to a darker kind, and soon he finds himself stalking the streets of London in search of random and innocent victims. He has become The Sandman.

'A truly remarkable insight into the workings of a deranged mind: a
vivid, extraordinarily powerful novel which will grip you to the end
and which you'll long remember' – *Mystery & Thriller Guild*
'A horribly deft piece of work!" – *Cosmopolitan*
'Written by a virtuoso – it luxuriates in death with a Jacobean fervour'
– *The Sydney Morning Herald*
'Confounds received notions of good taste – unspeakable acts are
reported with an unwavering reasonableness essential to the comic
impact and attesting to the deftness of Gibson's control.'
– *Times Literary Supplement*

ISBN 1 899344 24 1 – £7

The Do-Not Press
Fiercely Independent Publishing

Keep in touch with what's happening at the cutting edge of independent British publishing.

Join The Do-Not Press Information Service and receive advance information of all our new titles, as well as news of events and launches in your area, and the occasional free gift and special offer. Simply send your name and address to:

The Do-Not Press (Dept. LB)

PO Box 4215

London

SE23 2QD
or email us: thedonotpress@zoo.co.uk

There is no obligation to purchase and no salesman will call.

Visit our regularly-updated Internet site:

http://www.thedonotpress.co.uk

Mail Order

All our titles are available from good bookshops, or (in case of difficulty) direct from The Do-Not Press at the address above. There is no charge for post and packing. (NB: A postman may call.)